# BARKING AT A FOX-FUR COAT

# BARKING
## AT A
# FOX-FUR COAT

## DONALD DAVIS

*August House Publishers, Inc.*
LITTLE ROCK

Published by August House, Inc.,
P.O. Box 3223, Little Rock, Arkansas, 72203,
501-372-5450.

Printed in the United States of America

10 9 8 7 6 5 4 3 2 1

LIBRARY OF CONGRESS CATALOGING-IN-PUBLICATION DATA

Davis, Donald D., 1944–
Barking at a Fox-Fur Coat / Donald Davis. — 1st ed.
p.    cm.

ISBN 0-87483-141-5 (hb : acid-free paper) : $19.95
ISBN 0-87483-140-7 (pb : acid-free paper) : $9.95
1. Davis family—Folklore—Fiction.
2. Tales—North Carolina.  I. Title.
PS3554.A93347B37  1991
813'.54—dc20              91-27997

First Edition, 1991

Executive: Liz Parkhurst
Project editor: Judith Faust
Design director: Ted Parkhurst
Cover illustration and design: Kitty Harvill
Typography: Lettergraphics, Little Rock

This book is printed on archival-quality paper which meets the
guidelines for performance and durability of the Committee on
Production Guidelines for Book Longevity of the
Council on Library Resources.

AUGUST HOUSE, INC.        PUBLISHERS        LITTLE ROCK

*For Douglas, Kelly, and Jonathan*

# Preface and Acknowledgments

*A*lmost every family has at least a small stockpile of stories told by or about family members on the occasion of every family gathering. They are often called "those stories," meaning the ones Grandpa's told ten thousand times or the ones everybody tells about Uncle Ned.

Many such stories are prized as treasures by family members, and yet not shared beyond the family for fear that "no one else will understand." And it's true that sometimes the most important context of a story is its very lack of truth with respect to those who figure in it. Often there are reversals of character traits which we who are related to the protagonists enjoy very much—though we may also be sure that those involved would be embarrassed if these same stories were repeated elsewhere.

The result is a whole world full of wonderful stories which are seldom widely shared.

A distinguishing characteristic of such family stories is that they often span an unexamined gap between traditional storytelling and created fiction. That is, family stories often employ ancient traditional themes, placed not in the past nor with the traditional hero or heroine at their center but in a local setting populated by neighbors and family members. Jack becomes a lucky uncle and ancient Scotland the community just across the ridge.

From this appropriation of themes for local purposes, original fiction is but a short step. Often the sequel to the retold traditional story has become original in its entirety.

In the present collection, for example, the story "Uncle Frank Saves the Jollys," is built around two traditional fool themes found worldwide in traditional storytelling: the fools who have never seen the moon, and the separated fools who are convinced one is lost when the one counting the group does not count himself. In this instance, though, the world of the story, its places and characters, are wrought from the local world of the North Carolina mountains in which the story in its present form was born.

The sequel tale, "Whatever Happened to the Jollys," is original in its entirety. It is a story I "had" to come up with to explain what happened to all those characters (and to answer questions asked by listeners who thought they might have known a few folks like those in the story).

Each story found in this collection is part of this middle way between the spawning ground of the oral tradition and the finally achieved world of creative fiction.

In my own family, there were a wealth of such stories. Ours was a family in which traditional stories were carefully preserved and told—and a family in which original stories were often created on the spot. The in-between nature of these stories has become clearer and clearer to me in the years I have lived with them.

My present desire is to preserve and share them: first, as examples which might prompt the reader to remember and tell a long-neglected family story of his or her own; second, to show the way in which traditional storytellers interact with material and do not simply repeat stories by rote; and third, to point to the beginnings of creative fiction bred by familiarity with the tradition and long practice at the art of telling.

My great appreciation goes to many people for making this volume possible. To Ted and Liz Parkhurst at August House, I express my appreciation for support and understanding of storytelling which sensitively brings the oral to the print. My thanks in that regard also goes especially to Judith Faust, my editor there.

Within the storytelling community, thanks goes to four people. To Connie Regan-Blake and Barbara Freeman, who are responsible for asking me to tell a story "on purpose" for the first time; to my great friend Ed Stivender, who helped teach the Jollys to swim; and to Merle Smith Creech, whose reflections on my work constantly enlarge my perspective and possibilities.

My greatest appreciation goes to those family members whose thoughts and actual stories are the seeds for what I have put together here. Specific thanks are due to my father, Aunt Esther, Uncle Gudger, Aunt Kathleen, and to the memory of Aunt Mary, Uncle Grover, Uncle Lee, Uncle Harry, Uncle Moody, Aunt Flora, Uncle Mark, and especially, Uncle Frank.

# Contents

# Rainy Weather

*U*ncle Frank was a fox hunter. While he knew about fishing and squirrel hunting and coon hunting and all the rest, the sport of his life was fox hunting.

Many a night I left home with him before dark, a passel of foxhounds with us, to head up to a little building he had built on the peak of the ridge between Jolly Cove and the Crawfords' land.

On the outside wall of this small camping shelter built of framing timber and canvas was a great, hand-lettered sign: WORLD HEADQUARTERS: GREATER IRON DUFF FOX HUNTERS' ASSOCIATION, FRANK M. DAVIS, FOX-PRO.

Uncle Frank was not the founder of the Iron Duff Fox Hunters' Association. Their tradition was much longer even than his fox-hunting life. In those days, though, he was their leader: always an officer, always present, and of course, the one on whose farm the headquarters building was located.

Fox hunting in the southern mountains is not a violent sport. It is not even a sport in which human beings are involved in the pursuit. Southern fox hunting is a subtle sport of *listening*. It is, perhaps, more akin to music appreciation than to most other forms of hunting, in which the kill is the goal.

Once the hunters were installed in the open-sided headquarters building, Uncle Frank would let the dogs loose. They would circle and sniff until they picked up a trail, and then set off singing their barking songs in pursuit of the fox.

The point was not to catch the fox. The dogs' interest was to stay on the trail. The human hunters' interest was in listening to them sing as they did so.

Uncle Frank knew each hound by voice. "There goes old Belle," he would say, indicating a rapidly yelping dog off in the cove. "She must be running in the wet ground. She's got the longest toenails, and she can always outrun the rest of them in the wet ground."

"Over there's Warbler," he would say, indicating a dog who almost yodeled when he barked. "You'd never miss old Warbler!"

And so the night would go on—with, of course, a full bacon-and-egg midnight snack—as we listened to the dogs run and sing, lose the trail, pick it up, and run and sing again until they were worn out. Then we'd snooze a little before going on back to the house.

One night I said to Uncle Frank, "I'd like to be a real *dog-owning* fox hunter when I grow up, Uncle Frank...not just a visitor."

"Well, son," he replied, "you can't decide to do that."

"Why? Why can't I be a fox hunter?"

He cleared the matter up. "You *may* get to be a fox hunter, son. But you can't *decide* to be one. You see, fox hunting's a vocation. You have to have a *calling* to be a real fox hunter!"

"Well, I'll be called, then. How do I get called?" I asked, determined to be a fox hunter.

"Oh, that's not too hard." Uncle Frank's eyes were sparkling. "There are a lot of ways to be called. Why, one member of this club, who shall remain unnamed, was driving home from work one day when he started thinking about his wife, whom he was going home to. At that very moment, he got the call to fox hunt. There's lots of ways to get the call.

"The clearest call, I think, is heard by those who love the music of nature so much they just can't resist the song of those dogs on the trail of a fox. Listen to the music, son, and there's a good chance that you will get the call."

One of Uncle Frank's responsibilities as a perpetual officer of the Greater Iron Duff Fox Hunters' Association was to travel each year to the Pine Barrens of New Jersey for the National Foxhound Championship. He and one other officer of the club (usually Cousin Tom, since he had retired from the post office) would take Iron Duff's finest foxhound and enter him in the contest.

There in New Jersey, among the cranberry bogs, those great foxhounds gathered from across the nation would run in competition against one another. At the end of the three-day contest, two dogs would be crowned "Mister and Miz Foxhound, U.S.A." This was the highest honor that could come to any foxhound in America.

During this particular year, Uncle Frank and Cousin Tom headed north for New Jersey with Old Belle, the dog with the long toenails. They figured those long toenails might give her an advantage in the country around the cranberry bogs.

Belle ran well, but she did not win.

Uncle Frank and Tom were not too disappointed, though, because something else had captured their attention: the special featured guest of the competition.

Fishhook, an ancient dog, long senile and run down, was the foxhound Grand Marshal of Honor. The honor was his because he had been crowned "Mister Foxhound, U.S.A." seven years in a row—more times than any other dog in history.

Twenty-one years old now, Fishhook could no longer stand up, but he was comfortably nested in a polished walnut dog bed on a Sealy Posturepedic mattress made up with gold satin sheets. There was a little gold pillow under his chin to hold his head up, and there were six young lady dogs assigned just to wait on him and be sure that he had everything that he needed. Fishhook was a hound with a glorious past!

Uncle Frank and Cousin Tom looked him over, saw all his medals and ribbons, and read about his glorious past.

That night at their campsite, Uncle Frank and Cousin Tom got to talking about Fishhook.

"Do you know what, Frank?" Tom said, "My boy's in school down in Raleigh at State College, you know…"

"I know," Uncle Frank replied. "What do they call that subject he's studying…something about taking care of animals, isn't it?"

"Animal husbandry is what they call it," Tom said. "That's what I've been thinking about. Every time he comes home from Raleigh, he tells me about all the modern miracles of animal medical science. Why, one of these days, they're going to make a pig that's nothing but bacon and ham and a chicken than can lay two or three eggs a day!"

"I've read about some of that stuff," Uncle Frank put in. "I even hear some feller's working on an electric rooster. But what got you to thinking about it now, Tom?"

"Fishhook," Tom replied, almost in a whisper. "What I'm thinking is that you and I could buy that old dog— probably pretty cheap since he's got so much mileage on him—and my boy could *restore* him! I figure that even if his legs *are* shot, we could build him up enough to breed him. We could introduce an entirely new bloodline into the Iron Duff foxhounds!"

Uncle Frank, who had had the very same one himself, thought that was a fine idea. The two of them decided to give it a try.

The next day, they approached Fishhook's owner. There was nothing to it. The man had nursed the old dog all the way from Kentucky to the Pine Barrens of New Jersey, and he didn't figure Fishhook would live to make the trip back home again. He didn't really believe the dog would make it back to North Carolina with Uncle Frank and Cousin Tom, either. He threw in the mattressed walnut dog bed for good measure.

It was a slow and careful trip back to Iron Duff, but with plenty of rest stops, Uncle Frank and Cousin Tom made it just fine. Fishhook traveled well.

Cousin Tom wrote his son at State College to tell him about all the plans. The next time Tom Junior came home, he brought a big footlocker with him. He had cleaned out the closets at school and brought every experimental drug he could lay his hands on.

All the Iron Duff fox hunters joined in on the rejuvenation project.

They began to feed Fishhook a special high-protein, high-bulk, low-fat, cholesterol-free diet. They gave him witch hazel massages, end to end, three times a day. They gave him shots of hormones no one had ever even heard of.

They started on the vitamins: pills for all the ordinary-letter vitamins A through K, with double doses of vitamin E. A series of shots for all the B-vitamins: B-12, B-13, B-14—all the way up to and including B-29! (They were determined to make a bomber out of him!)

Gradually, as this work went on, Fishhook was coming back to his old life. His appetite picked up; his disposition improved; his whole outlook about the future became more positive.

Pretty soon he was able to get up and walk around. Not long after that, he began to show an interest when he heard the other dogs barking at night. By the time he got his B-29

shot, he was scratching at the door, begging to go out and
chase foxes with the other dogs.

"No, Fishhook." Uncle Frank held him back. "You
can't chase foxes, especially not on these dark nights. We've
just got too much invested in you. Besides, you have been
restored for a higher calling!"

Pretty soon, old Fishhook seemed to be about as young
as he was going to get, and the debate arose about which of
the female dogs he should be mated with.

All the Iron Duff fox hunters who had any kind of
female dog at all quickly volunteered, but Uncle Frank held
firm. His mind was made up. Old Belle was to be the one.
He figured that with those long toenails she could keep her
footing better and Fishhook would have a better chance of
being successful.

And so the great day arrived.

Uncle Frank had kept Belle up for three days in a row
so she would be all rested. He had a little fatherly talk with
her about how they had restored Fishhook's body, but they
weren't so sure about his memory—she might have to help
him out with remembering a few things.

Old Belle and the new Fishhook were put in a little dog
lot on the hill above Uncle Frank's house and left in privacy
for the afternoon. Pretty soon, the pleasant sounds which
rose into the air seemed to indicate that Fishhook's memory
was at least as good as his body.

"I believe they know what they're doing," Tom told
Uncle Frank.

Then, all of a sudden, from inside the dog lot a terrible
sound was heard: *Yeeeeooooowww!* Then, *Thump,* something hit the ground.

Uncle Frank and the other assembled members of the
Iron Duff Fox Hunter's Association were almost afraid to
open the gate. Still, the truth had to be faced.

Slowly they opened the gate to the dog lot and looked inside.

There was Belle against the back fence. She was standing stock still and seemed to be trembling a little. In the center of the lot, flat on his back on the ground, lay Fishhook, as Uncle Frank said later, "dead as a door nail."

They never knew what killed him, technically speaking. Dr. York came and looked him over, but he really couldn't tell anything. "Could have been a heart attack...could have been a stroke...it was pretty surely some kind of a blowout." Beyond that speculation, no one knew.

It was sad when old (again!) Fishhook was buried. Not only was it sad to see him go, but also there was the great loss of hope that had been placed in his mating with Belle, hope, now gone, for a new bloodline in the Iron Duff foxhounds. These were days of sadness.

A few weeks later, however, spirits soared. Suddenly it became evident that in that last great calling of his life, Fishhook had been effective. Belle was indeed going to have pups!

To hear Uncle Frank tell it, no woman in Iron Duff had ever been cared for the way that mother dog was spoiled during the coming weeks. She was confined to the barn and waited on hand and foot. As her time drew near, a special labor room was set up in one of the feed rooms, and the members of the Greater Iron Duff Fox Hunters' Association signed on to sit with her in shifts around the clock.

On a cold, rainy night in March, just before four o'clock in the morning, Belle's pups were born.

Except it was not "pups." It was just "pup."

Out of all that hard work, out of all that expense, out of all that time and effort and hope, Belle had had just one pup.

But he was perfect! Beautifully shaped and marked, the little dog seemed to be a natural-born champion. Because of the night on which he was born, Uncle Frank named him "Rainy Weather."

Rainy Weather was a prodigy of natural fox-hound talent. Before he was old enough to stand and walk, he would roll his head around and sniff the air in a particular direction and when Uncle Frank let the big dogs loose later, that would be exactly the direction in which they ran. Little Rainy Weather was smelling the fox scent, with all the doors and windows shut, before he was big enough to walk.

As the little dog grew up, the stories about him became legion. People would say, "Rainy Weather? Why, that dog can smell with his nose taped up," and "Mr. Davis has got a dog can smell fox tracks under water!" Everybody in Iron Duff was talking about Rainy Weather! And as he grew, he did indeed become a fabulous foxhound.

Of course, all the members of the Greater Iron Duff Fox Hunters' Association had very *important* thoughts on their minds. They knew that when Rainy Weather got to be two years old, they could send him up to New Jersey as the Iron Duff entrant in the National Foxhound Championship, and they were all sure he was a cinch to be "Mister Foxhound, U. S. A."

All the hunters did was watch him develop. There was no training to it. Rainy Weather knew by instinct exactly what to do before any suggestion could be offered by man or dog. It was just a matter of time until fame would be coming to Iron Duff.

Uncle Frank and Cousin Tom began to get ready to take Rainy Weather to New Jersey.

A few arrangements had to be made before they could leave. Uncle Frank did, after all, milk and feed about forty cows, and they all had to be milked and fed while he was gone. He usually had a dairyman on the farm to help out, but his last dairyman had quit and he hadn't hired a new one. He was going to have to hunt up some temporary help.

That was the problem. Most people in Iron Duff had about all of their own work they could keep up with, and so the only people available for temporary employment were the subnatural Jolly boys.

Uncle Frank went up in the cove to Phyleete and Wife Jolly's house and hired Lizard and Clogger. He brought them down to the dairy and took them into the feed room of the big barn to teach them what had to be done while he was gone.

It was slow going with Clogger because he literally took every heavy step twice, but he was dependable. He was a great big overgrown boy now and wore number-twelve brogans on his feet. When those gunboat feet double-stepped into the feed room at the big barn, the old board floor just wouldn't hold and Clogger stomped his way right through it!

"The ground's let me down again!" Clogger cried out.

"Aw, Clogger," Uncle Frank said, "That's not the ground. That's just the old, rotten floor of the feed room. You stomped your way through the floor! Now you're *standing* on the ground. Look."

Uncle Frank began to pull the broken boards out of the way until he, Lizard, and Clogger could clearly see that Clogger *was* now standing flat on the ground about six or eight inches below where the floor used to be.

Suddenly, even in the dim light of the feed room, they all saw the same thing at once.

There in the dirt under the floor of the old barn's feed room was a clearly visible set of fox tracks.

"Look, Mr. Davis," cried Lizard, "fox tracks! How did a fox get under the floor?"

Uncle Frank realized what they were looking at. "The fox didn't get under the floor, boys. It couldn't. Why, that fox had to have come through here and left those tracks before this barn was ever built!"

"How long ago was that?" Lizard asked.

"Let's see...the barn has been here just about sixty years. I remember Daddy building it when I was a little boy. Those tracks have to be at least that old, and I guess they could be a whole lot older than that!"

"Go get Rainy Weather, Mr. Davis," Clogger begged.

"How come, Clogger?" Uncle Frank asked.

"See if he can foller that fox. Why, you know he can. Those tracks are clear as can be, and old Rainy Weather can foller tracks he can't even see at all!"

"Foxhounds follow by smell, Clogger. They don't have to *see* tracks, but they do have to *smell* them. And I can surely guarantee you that sixty-year-old fox tracks...well, they may look good, but they surely don't have any smell left in them." Uncle Frank thought that ought to make some sense to the Jollys, but it didn't.

"Aw, let him try," begged Lizard.

"Yeah, let him try," Clogger joined in. "It won't hurt to let him try!"

They wouldn't give up. They begged and annoyed Uncle Frank until he finally realized that nothing would convince the Jolly boys until they could see for themselves. He might as well let Rainy Weather have a useless and unfruitful sniff and get this over with.

While Uncle Frank went to get the dog, Lizard and Clogger cleared more of the boards away, until when Uncle Frank returned with Rainy Weather in tow, a good long set of fox tracks was visible.

Suddenly Rainy Weather caught sight of those fox tracks. He yelped twice, jumped into the air, jerked loose from Uncle Frank, and, nose to the ground, took off after that fox that had passed through Iron Duff at least sixty years ago!

Getting started was the hard part. Rainy Weather jumped down through that hole that Clogger had stomped in the feed room floor. He wiggled on his belly following those tracks along under that low-to-the-ground floor. When he came to the foundation of the barn, he dug his way under, then broke free into the feed lot, running and yelping for all he was worth.

"Look at him go, Mr. Davis!" Lizard exclaimed. He knew all the time that Rainy Weather could do it.

Uncle Frank stood open-mouthed and silent as Rainy Weather went out of the barnyard and right into a big corn field, following the scent of that very fox which had been long gone for well over half a century.

Rainy Weather was tearing that corn field up. He was knocking corn down and throwing dirt every which way.

"Why's he acting like that?" Lizard asked. "How come he don't just run up and down the rows?"

"Oh, Lizard," Uncle Frank answered, "that cornfield wasn't there sixty years ago. This was all woodland back then. Rainy Weather's just having to run around the trees like that fox did! Besides, boys, as many times as that field's been plowed during all the years since, he's having an awful time digging all those tracks back up and getting them in the right order!"

In a few minutes, Rainy Weather had crossed the cornfield, broken out on the lower side, and started smelling and yelping his way across the lower-cove cow pasture. The dog would run straight for a while, jump sort of sideways in the air, then hit the ground and run some more. This odd jumping and running went on all across the cow pasture.

"How come he's jumping all around like that?" Clogger asked. "Ain't no reason for nobody to git *that* far above the ground!"

"I've got that just figured out, Clogger," Uncle Frank assured him. "Years ago there was a fence row running right through where that pasture is now. Tore it out when I made the pasture bigger. Rainy Weather is having to jump over where that fence used to be every time that old fox jumped it back when it was still there. He's following the fox trail right through the air!"

It was amazing.

About then Rainy Weather came to a place where there had been a hole in the fence. The fox had without a doubt gone through that hole. Now, sniffing and following the trail, Rainy Weather tried to follow. Only trouble was that when the hole had been there, it hadn't been big enough for Rainy Weather to get through.

He hit the place where the hole had been and stuck right there in midair, wiggling and kicking. Everybody thought he was going to have to back up and go around, but he wiggled and kicked until he enlarged the place where the old hole had been and finally made it big enough so he could get through it.

After that, Uncle Frank, Lizard, and Clogger got to worrying. They saw Rainy Weather running full speed with his nose to the ground, headed straight toward the Flat Field. Except the Flat Field wasn't there any more. The Flat Field was where Uncle Frank had built the new pond. There Rainy Weather went, running and barking, straight toward the water.

That dog hit the edge of the pond and went straight to the bottom! On he went, out of sight, underwater, following the trail of that fox right across the bottom of the pond!

Of course, when Rainy Weather went under the water, they couldn't hear him barking. The quiet did not last for long, though, as in a matter of seconds, bubbles began to come to the top of the water. Every time one of those bubbles popped, a little bark came out of it! The bubble-barks made a trail on top of the water which marked Rainy Weather's progress all the way across the bottom of the fish pond.

Rainy Weather's mother, Old Belle, had passed her long toenails along to her wonderful offspring. With those long toenails digging into the soft bottom of the pond, Rainy Weather was able to keep his speed up, even under water!

In fact, when he broke out of the water and was running on dry land again on the other side, he had left the water so fast that he had outrun a whole bunch of bubbles, and as they slowly rose to the top of the water and popped, it sounded for a brief time like two dogs barking at once: real barks and bubble-barks, back and forth, back and forth, until the bubbles ran out and Rainy Weather was just barking on his own again.

Uncle Frank, Lizard, and Clogger stood there and listened while Rainy Weather barked his way up through the Jolly Cove and out of sight over the ridge above the World Headquarters building.

Suddenly all the barking stopped.

"What's happened to him?" Lizard asked. "He's stopped!"

"Oh, I don't think he's stopped," Uncle Frank answered. "You see, once he crossed that ridge above the fox hunting house, he was onto Sam Crawford's land. Sam's got a bunch of 'No Trespassing' signs up over there, and Rainy Weather knows not to bark when he reads one of them. We'll hear him again in a little while."

Sure enough, it wasn't long until Rainy Weather started barking again.

And so they listened to Rainy Weather bark, following the sixty-year-old fox scent, as he ran over the top of the Kansada Mountain and faded from earshot.

A good foxhound will sometimes stay on a trail until completely exhausted. Some dogs just will not give up until they fall over on the ground, and still they struggle to bark, even when they can run no more. It was no surprise, then, when Rainy Weather had not come home at the end of the day. Uncle Frank just figured he had run until his legs gave out, and that the dog would either come home in the morning or some neighbor would spot him and call for Uncle Frank to come get him.

The next day, Rainy Weather did not come home. Up in the afternoon, Uncle Frank got on the phone and called all the neighbors to see if anyone knew where he was. Several people had spotted him (or heard him and recognized his voice) headed west. Uncle Frank tracked Rainy Weather by telephone over into Jonathan's Creek, then Cataloochee, and finally on to Cosby, Tennessee, but there he lost him.

The next day, he got in his truck and drove all around that part of the country looking, talking to people, asking about signs of Rainy Weather. But the dog was nowhere to be found.

All the members of the Greater Iron Duff Fox Hunters' Association and many of their family members formed a search party. They divided up into a telephone committee, a dirt road committee, a paved road committee, a posted land committee, and an Interstate 40 committee, all searching high and low for Rainy Weather. But he had simply vanished.

Uncle Frank and Tom had to cancel their trip to New Jersey. The National Foxhound Championship came and went, and for the first time in memory, no one representing Iron Duff was there.

Back in Iron Duff, there was a time of mourning and great sadness among all the fox hunters. The best dog they had ever known was gone, and that was that. Finally Uncle Frank suggested they all just put Rainy Weather out of mind and get back to living in the present.

Days passed, then weeks. If not forgotten, at least Rainy Weather was no longer talked about. On the surface of things, Iron Duff fox hunting returned to normal.

Nearly three months passed. Early one morning, Uncle Frank was returning to the house after the morning feeding and milking. When he opened the kitchen door, the telephone was ringing.

He hurried to the phone, picked it up, and said hello to the early caller.

"Hello," replied a strange voice. "Is this Mr. Frank Davis?"

"Yes it is, in person," Uncle Frank answered.

"Do you live in some place called Iron Duff, North Carolina?"

"Yes, I do," Uncle Frank said. "Could you tell me who's calling?"

"This is the Chief of Police in Baltimore, Maryland," the voice replied.

"You don't say!" Uncle Frank had never talked to a big-city police chief before. "What can I do for you?"

"Well, Mr. Davis, *I'm* the one who may be able to do something for *you.* Let me see where to start... Mr. Davis, have you lost a dog?"

Lost a dog? Uncle Frank couldn't believe his ears. "Why yes, I lost a dog...must have been three months ago...he was..."

The Chief cut him off in mid-thought. "Listen, Mr. Davis, this morning we had a call about a break-in. It was down in a pretty tough part of town close to the inner harbor. Not much around there but pawn shops, beer joints, and secondhand stores."

"What's this all about?" Uncle Frank's patience was waning.

"Mr. Davis, somebody had broken the front window out of a used-clothing store, set off the burglar alarm and everything. We sent two cars to the scene of the presumed crime. When they got there, they went inside to investigate. Nobody had touched the cash register; nobody had made a mess of anything; nobody had taken a thing. They couldn't figure it out."

Uncle Frank just listened.

"Then they heard a noise. Something was making an awful racket way back in the back of the store—that's the bargain department where they keep all of the real worn-out stuff.

"They went back there, Mr. Davis, with their guns drawn, and when they got there, what they found was *your dog*, barking at an old, worn-out fox-fur coat! He was so hoarse you could hardly understand him."

Uncle Frank was silent with amazement.

"We got your address off of his collar. Do you want him back?"

Uncle Frank had recovered his speech by now, and he answered, "Of course, I want him back. He's the finest dog I ever had. How do I go about getting him home again?"

"We've already checked that out," the Chief replied. "The Trailways bus won't take him. We'll have to fly him back. That means we have to get an escort to take him to the airport, pay for what they call a 'sky kennel'... Well, Mr. Davis, all together, it's going to cost over two hundred dollars to get your dog back."

"That sure is a lot of money," Uncle Frank seemed to think out loud. "How much is that fox-fur coat?"

"I don't know about that," the Chief replied. "Let me ask the man that owns the place. I think he's still here at the station. Just hold on a minute."

Uncle Frank waited. The Chief came back to the phone.

"The owner says that old coat could be forty, maybe fifty years old. Says he's bought and sold it a half-dozen times. He'll sell it to you for ten dollars plus postage just to get rid of it."

"Kathleen's been wanting a coat like that for a long time," was Uncle Frank's reply. "I'll tell you what. I can't afford to have that dog sent back, not for two hundred dollars, but I'll send you the ten dollars if you'll send me that coat. Just do whatever you have to with that dog!"

And so Rainy Weather was taken to the Baltimore dog pound, and that ancient, well-traveled and well-worn fox-fur coat went in the U.S. Mail, parcel post, to Aunt Kathleen.

About a week later, Uncle Frank heard a noise coming down the road. It was the mailman's car, and about twenty yards behind, there came old Rainy Weather, nose to the ground, still barking with every step.

At the next meeting of the Greater Iron Duff Fox Hunter's Association, Rainy Weather was given a retirement party. It was decided that he didn't need to go to the National Foxhound Championship, or anywhere else, for that matter, because he was already "Mister Foxhound, U.S.A."

# Uncle Frank and the Southern Bells

*N*o matter what many outsiders might think about life in the North Carolina mountains, we did have many modern conveniences when I was growing up in Haywood County. We had electricity (after the Tennessee Valley Authority came through, people had electricity who didn't have anything to plug in), we had running water, and we had a radio station.

But for most people, there was no telephone service available except right in the middle of town.

We got our first telephone when I was six years old.

The "Southern Bells" had come to town and installed a modern telephone system, and for the first time, the general public could get a telephone outside the city limits of downtown Waynesville.

Our number was one-two-nine. Mother was so fascinated with learning to use the new telephone that I stayed home from school for three days to watch (and listen to) how that thing worked before she ever noticed I wasn't going to school.

This was no old-time wooden crank-phone either. No, the Southern Bells were modern in every way. Our telephone looked like a big, black daffodil with an extra cup hanging on the side of it. To make a call, I observed, all you had to do was pick up the cup and hold it to your ear.

In a moment a strange woman's voice would say, "Number, please!" and all you had to do then was tell that black daffodil who you wanted to talk to. (Using names worked much better than knowing the numbers. If people weren't at their own number and you asked for them by name, the operator seemed to know just where to find them anyway!)

Uncle Frank was terribly jealous about our telephone. The Southern Bells didn't run lines all the way out to Iron Duff, and so he couldn't get one. Every time he came to our house, he wanted to play with that telephone.

He would drive right past stores that were open for business, come to our house, and call them on the telephone to ask whether they had this or that. Sometimes he'd ask about things I knew he could have seen right in the store windows as he drove by. He would circle around through town and spot cars to see who was at home so he could call them to see if they were well and getting along all right. He loved to use the telephone.

"I can't wait until I can get one of these things," he would say. "A telephone could save half of my trips to town. Why, if I could only get a telephone, I'd save so much time that I'd get a lot more work done on the farm. Keep up with things better, too!"

It took four more years for the Southern Bells to run the telephone lines all the way to Iron Duff. Then, at last, Uncle Frank got his telephone.

His new telephone number was four-three-one-R. The notice from the Southern Bells containing this information stated that the "R" stood for "Rural," but when he told us his new number, Uncle Frank explained that the "R" stood for "Rare!"

There was one problem with the new telephone: way out there in Iron Duff, the only service Uncle Frank could get hooked into was an eight-party line—eight households on one telephone line!

In itself, the eight-party line was no problem. After all, Uncle Frank did have a busy farm to run and certainly did not want to use the telephone all the time, just for important information and emergencies.

The *real* problem was that two of the eight parties on the eight-party line were two past-middle-age unmarried sisters—Miss Lucy and Miss Lena Leatherwood. Once the Leatherwood sisters were connected by the Southern Bells, nobody else on that line had a chance!

Every time Uncle Frank picked up the phone, the Leatherwood sisters were talking: "Yap, yap, yap...yap, yap, yap..."

He paid his bill from the Southern Bells at the end of the first month, and he had never made even one call on his telephone.

On his next visit to our house, Uncle Frank was all fired up about Miss Lucy's and Miss Lena's monopolization of the telephone line.

"They're not getting dressed," he said. "They can't be. They're not staying off the phone long enough to put their clothes on. And something else: they're going to starve to death. I just know they are. I can pick up the phone at breakfast time, at dinner time, at supper time, and all they ever do with their mouths is talk. They are going to starve to death!"

The next time he came to our house, Daddy asked him, "Frank, have the Leatherwood sisters starved to death yet?"

There was an edge of disappointment to his voice as he reported: "No, they're not going to starve to death. I can hear one of them eating while the other one talks!"

Uncle Frank paid his Southern Bells bill for the second month. He had still never made the first call on his telephone.

Once in a while, a stranger, hearing of these events, would look puzzled. "Why?" such an uninformed person might ask Uncle Frank. "Why do the Leatherwood sisters *need* telephones? I mean, two unmarried sisters...why do they have two houses to start with? Why don't they just both live at the old family home place?"

Uninformed strangers (and even some ignorant local folks) were due an explanation, which Uncle Frank readily supplied.

"It's like this," I heard him tell one such questioner, "Miss Lucy was *married* for a little while. Not even long enough for people to learn to call her by her husband's name, but she *was* married." Then the whole story unfolded.

It seems that when she was about fifty-five years old, Miss Lucy met a neighbor, Mr. Bob Chambers.

Mr. Bob was sixty-seven years old and also never married. He told people he was "saving it for retirement," whatever that meant.

Mr. Bob had a good-sized farm, a small herd of white-faced cattle, and thirty-seven beehives. He began to think he did want to slow things down a bit, but he didn't want to give up farming altogether. He decided the best thing for him to do was to take on some help.

He did not chart his course lightly. He, as he said, "studied on it."

"About the best and quickest way I've seen to get free help," he said, reporting on his research, "seems to be to just get married." And so, he went shopping.

The market in prospective working brides for sixty-seven year-old men was not great in Iron Duff. About the *only* possibilities he could come up with were the Leather-wood sisters. He went up to see the two of them and explained his proposition.

Miss Lena ran him off, but Miss Lucy ran after him. She caught him before he was far down the road, accepted his offer, and within a very short time, they were married.

Miss Lucy packed up all her belongings and hauled them about a mile down the road to Mr. Bob's house and moved in with her new husband, leaving her sister Lena at the old home place all alone.

One week from the day of their marriage, Mr. Bob died.

People would look at one another, mention Mr. Bob's untimely death, and get silly-looking half-grins on their faces. "Reckon what killed him just a week after he got married?" someone would ask. Nobody answered. They just tried not to grin too big.

That confused me. I was accustomed to seeing people look sad when someone was dead. To see folks blush, then smile, as they mused about the cause of Mr. Bob's demise made no sense to me at all. I decided I should ask my mother about it.

At breakfast the next morning, I raised the question. "Mama, reckon what killed Mr. Bob just a week..."

I was rudely cut off in the middle of my question by a sharp slap across my face. I not only got no answer, I also got no breakfast.

I might have been hurt and hungry, but my curiosity was whetted. Now I just had to know what had happened. Maybe it was time to ask Aunt Esther. She always knew the answer to everything.

Next time I was at her house, I did. "Aunt Esther," (I was ready to duck in a hurry this time in case her answer was the same as my mother's), "what do you reckon killed Mr. Bob just a week after he and Miss Lucy got married?"

She stopped what she was doing and looked at me wistfully. "I am not a doctor, son," she said, "but I have thought about it." Then under her breath she added, "I guess everybody has." I awaited her answer.

"I think," the answer was coming now, "I think that he must have succumbed to an extreme overdose of unaccustomed affection."

There it was, and I didn't know what *that* meant either Sounded like some kind of medical terminology to me, but whatever it was, it killed him!

So Miss Lucy was left in her newly inherited home (which people said she had earned in a week), while her sister remained at their family homeplace back up the road.

This explained why these unmarried sisters didn't live together and needed the Southern Bells telephone line to hook them up.

Uncle Frank paid his bill for the third month straight, and *still* he had not been able to make a single call on his telephone.

If you have ever been on one of those party lines, you know what it is like to find someone (usually the same someone) talking every single time you pick up the phone to make a call. And while no one in Haywood County would ever consider actually and deliberately *listening in* on someone else's private conversation (Uncle Frank certainly wouldn't), it might be that you thought if you listened *just a minute,* you could perhaps get an idea about how long the present party might be on. This was, of course, only in the interest of estimating when it would be your turn to make a call.

Uncle Frank did admit that once in a while he might listen *just a minute* to the Leatherwood sisters—just to see how long they might be expected to talk, of course. (After three months, he was surely due *one* chance to talk.) Considering the speed at which the Leatherwood sisters could exchange words, he could actually hear quite a bit in one of those minutes!

He once told us about picking up his telephone one evening just as Miss Lucy was getting wound up to fill her sister in on her activities of the day:

"It was them vity-mine pills that done it—made me sick as a dog—I got up this morning feeling swimmy-headed—shaky, shaky, shaky all over—called Miz Galloway on the telephone and said to her that I was feeling swimmy-headed—shaky, shaky, shaky all over—she says for me to get something to eat and I'll feel better—I told her I had already had something to eat and I didn't feel no better—she says what did I have—I told her I had a big cup of coffee with four spoons of sugar in it and a big old Hershey bar and a big Co-Cola and I was just as shaky, shaky, shaky as I was before I ate anything—I said for her to come and get me and take me to see Dr. Lancaster—she pulled up in front of the house in a little while in that big old blue Pontiac of hers and I got in the car with her—I didn't know that she couldn't drive atall—she just run back and forth and back and forth all over the road and into one ditch and out of it and over into the other one—I thought that law I was going to get killed before we ever got to town and as sick as I was I wasn't in no shape to die before I ever got to see the doctor—we got to town and she pulled up there in front on the Masonic Temple there where all of them doctors' offices are and we got out and went in the door—there was one of them little elly-vaters inside of the door and she says to let's get in that elly-vater and I says that I ain't going to get in no little box that goes up and down and you don't never know where you're a-going to come out of it let's go up the stairs—she says she can't go up the stairs on account of she has got too much gout in her legs—I says she is the one who ought to go to see the doctor and she says that she is going to go as soon as the gout goes down out of her legs—so we get in that little elly-vater and she goes to punching buttons and we go up and down and up and down and up and down and we come out right where we started—we get back in there and this time I go to punching and we come out somewhere else and we figure this is the right place because there is a sign sticking out of the wall on down the hall that says Doctor Lancaster and that is his office I bet—we go on in there and out comes Miss Winnie Kirkpatrick that little nurse and she says do I have any appoint-ment and I say I do not have no appointment in that I did not make no plan on being sick—and she says I will just have to sign up and wait and I sign up and wait—people come and they went and they come and they went and some of them was sick when they come and some of them was sick when they went and some of them had one thing when they come and before they had went they had done got over that and left out of there with something else—and about five o'clock she says the doctor will look at me now and I go into a little room where he comes in another hour or two—he says to me to take off my clothes and I say to him no sir no sir I did not come in here for nothing like that and he says I will just have to let Miss Winnie look at me then—and she gets me in the same little room and pokes me all over and looks inside of me and outside of me and all over me and then she says she don't see nothing wrong with me—and I say I wouldn't either if had looked where she did—and she says for me to just go back out there and let the doctor talk to me and he does and he gives me a big jar of vity-mine pills and he says there is nothing wrong with me except I have been drinking too many Co-Colas and not taking no vity-mine pills and that I ought to take one the first chance I get and another one the next chance I get and one just about ever chance I get and quit drinking so many Co-Colas—me and Miz Galloway come out of there and it was plumb dark and we hadn't had nothing to eat all of the whole blessed day and I say for us to stop at Charlie's

Drive-In so we can get us some sam-wiches and we pull in there and I get me two foot-long hot dogs with mustard and chili and onions all over them and a big plate of fried 'taters and a big old Pepsi-Coler—cause I ain't on the doctor's orders s'pose to drink Co-Colas no more—and I take two of them vity-mine pills and eat them hot-dogs and take two more of them vity-mine pills and eat some of them fried 'taters and take two more of them vity-mine pills and drink me a Pepsi-Coler and Miz Galloway starts in to driving back toward home and we are hitting them curves below Lake Junaluska and them vity-mine pills starts to jumping on me and I say I am a-going to be sick and she says to roll down the window and I say I have got it rolled down and she says for me to stick my head out and I say I have done got my head stuck out as for as I can and she says for me to blow and I blowed—I blowed them hot-dogs and 'taters all down the side of the Pigeon River—lost over two dollars worth of food—don't you never take none of them vity-mine pills, them things will go to jumping and kill you..."

*Clunk,* Uncle Frank's minute was up. He told us later that if he had had one more minute, it would have been educational to listen to her sister give a second opinion, but he had to get up early to milk and so he needed to go to bed.

My mother would say, "Frank, you shouldn't do that!"

"Well, listen to this," he said. "The other day I came in the house and picked up the phone, and one of them said to the other one '...burnt their house to the ground!'"

Mother's ears pricked up. "Whose house was it?"

"I don't know," he answered. "I listened for about forty-five minutes, and they talked about everything from strike-anywhere matches to 'outlawing faulted thermy-stats,' but I never did hear them say whose house it was."

Mother was disappointed.

Uncle Frank paid his bill for the *fourth* month of sup-posed telephone service. He knew you could hear on that thing, but he had not actually had even one chance to find out whether you could talk on it or not!

Then one morning just after milking, Uncle Frank went into the kitchen and picked up the phone just for a "telephone check." To his astonishment, there was complete silence instead of all of that "yap, yap, yap."

A strange voice said, "Number, Please."

Now, most people with no more experience than Uncle Frank wouldn't have known what to do at that moment, but, as he told us later, he had had *four months* to think about it. He didn't even hesitate.

"Just give me Miss Lucy Leatherwood's number, please!"

"She's on your party line, sir," the operator said, as if Uncle Frank didn't know that all too well. "You'll have to hang up. Then I'll start both of your phones to ringing, and when yours stops, you pick it up, and she'll be right there!"

Uncle Frank did as he was told. He placed the earpiece back on the telephone hook and waited. His telephone barely went "Ding!" before it stopped ringing. He picked up the receiver, and he could hear her hollering before he even got it to his ear. "Lena? Lena?"

"Miss Leatherwood," Uncle Frank began in a low and serious voice, "this is not your sister Lena."

"Well, who is it then?" she sounded like she could not imagine anyone else possibly being on *her* phone line!

Uncle Frank was taken aback. "Who is it?" he repeated. (He hadn't thought about being asked that!)

He pondered for just a moment and then answered confidently. "Miss Leatherwood, this is Mr. Bell. I am one of the Southern Bells. I am calling you from our headquarters up here in town to warn you about a potential problem you may have with your telephone..."

"Problem?" she interrupted, sounding panicky. "I can't have a problem. I haven't even talked to my sister yet at all this morning, and I don't know whether she woke up dead or alive or what all..."

Uncle Frank broke in. "Now listen! Look around and tell me, Miss Leatherwood, is there anything in the room in which your telephone is located which could be damaged by a large, sudden volume of water?"

"O Lord, yes," she replied in a distressed tone of voice. "There's a Persian rug that came from my mama and a sideboard that came from my grandmama and a pie safe that came from my daddy's Aunt Mable and a grandfather clock that came from my..."

Uncle Frank cut her off again. "Listen! You may be in danger! There was a big thunderstorm last night up in the Bowlegged Valley, thunder and lightning thrashing around everywhere. Well, about two o'clock this morning, a big bolt of lightning hit the main telephone pole above the Pigeon River and knocked it smack down. The lines sagged way low down over the river.

"We sent some men out there this morning to try to put a new pole back up, and while they were trying to do that, those telephone lines *busted* and fell in the river.

"When that happens, Miss Leatherwood, those lines will go to sucking water. It wouldn't be such a problem if you had those little *private* lines out there, but Miss Leatherwood, those big *eight*-party lines will suck about forty gallons a minute.

"Why, there was a man up by the Antioch Church who answered his telephone a little while ago, and before he could hang that thing up, the water broke his glasses, washed his teeth out of his mouth, drowned his cat, put out the fire in his cookstove, and backed up nine inches deep in the floor!

"Miss Leatherwood...*don't use your telephone!*

"You can swim, can't you?"

"Why, no," she said. "My sister and I neither one ever learned to swim! What will happen to us?"

"Well, if I were you, I'd put my telephone in a big tub—just to give you a running start in case someone gets a wrong number. Don't worry, though. The Southern Bells will let you know when it's okay to use that thing again!"

As soon as Miss Lucy hung up, Uncle Frank got down to business. He called Daddy and Uncle Grover and Aunt Jessie and Uncle Gudger and Aunt Mary and Uncle Lee and Aunt Pat and Uncle Moody and Aunt Rebekah and Uncle Harry and Aunt Zula and Aunt Flora—why, before the day was over, he said, he was calling people who weren't even related to him, making up for four months on that telephone!

The next morning he was going to call a few more people, but when he picked up his telephone, the line was dead.

He got in his car and drove toward town, looking for the problem. He found it. As he passed the Leatherwood sister's two houses, he could see that each had her telephone hanging out a window so it could safely drain outside on the ground.

And so, knowing that if you can't talk, being able to listen is better than nothing, Uncle Frank persuaded my mother to write two letters to the Leatherwood sisters from the Southern Bells explaining that everything was all dried out now, and they could go back to using their telephones.

# Uncle Frank Saves the Jollys

*T*he first of our family came from Wales. One Thomas Davis (or perhaps in the homeland it had been "Davies"), an immigrant whose exact place and date of origin are not further known, eventually made his way, after immigration, from Virginia to North Carolina.

At some unspecified time (generally noted as "after the Revolutionary War," or "before 1800," or "after 1800," which covers most of the options), the first of this Thomas Davis's descendants established themselves in what later became Haywood County, North Carolina.

Our great-great-(nobody really knows exactly how far back)-great-grandfather settled beside the Pigeon River in an area which later was politically domesticated as "Iron Duff in Haywood County."

He had fought (briefly) in the Revolutionary War, for which service he received two North Carolina land grants. The granting documents delineated two points on the Pigeon River and bestowed on him, between those two points, "all the land from the Pigeon River west." Period!

My brother and I often lamented the great wealth that should have been ours as owners of a great, endless slice of land which came to include not only Knoxville, Nashville, and Memphis but also Oklahoma City, Santa Fe, Las Vegas, Monterey Bay, and fishing rights to a good chunk of the Pacific Ocean. Our wealth was stolen, however, by an inventor named John Sevier. He is remembered for creating out of sheer and utter nothingness a thing he called "Tennessee." In 1796, he set up his invention on the western slope of *our* mountains and cut off our family's future path to true nationwide prominence.

Great-great-(plus or minus a great or two)-grandfather lived there beside the Pigeon River and spent most of his leisure time watching other people as they passed.

Those traveling west had come a long way to get this far. Families starting out as far away as New York and Pennsylvania would try to head west, only to run smack into the barrier of the Appalachian Mountains. They would turn south, hoping the mountains would eventually run out and they might simply go around. The mountains kept going, though, and by the time they got to North Carolina, travelers either jumped right in and headed through the Appalachians toward Tennessee or simply degenerated and populated South Carolina.

Those who plowed on west over the mountains found themselves following the Pigeon River past Great-great-plus-or-minus-grandfather's house, and he found himself well entertained.

It was a great parade. Some people seemed to have gradually lost their worldly possessions until they were down to what they carried on their backs. Others, perhaps by picking up what earlier travelers had dropped or thrown away, accumulated their way into a strung-out family wagon train. Either extreme was a fascination to rest your eyes on.

Some of the passersby looked so pitiful that our benevolent ancestor appealed to them to stop and rest for a while.

"I've got plenty of land," he would say (though after the John Sevier invention, the family grant was down to barely two thousand acres), "and you look pitiful! Why don't you just stop here and rest for a while.

"Build yourself a little log house, have a baby, sleep late, fatten up—after all that, you can even take a bath. Then in a year or two, when you're feeling back to normal, you can go on west and find your own land."

Many families did just that. When my brother and I were small, Daddy and Uncle Frank would walk us over the farm and show us the fallen-down remains of log cabins which had housed these transient squatters. Often all that was left was a tumble of rocks from a fallen chimney and an apple tree or grape vine.

One day, a family came by that looked considerably worse than usual. Great-great-plus-or-minus-grandfather invited them to stop, and they never did move on. They were the first Jollys in Iron Duff.

"What did they do?" I asked Uncle Frank.

"Well, son," he replied, "they just sort of laid up around in there and proliferated."

"What does that mean?"

"I can't directly tell you, son. You're not old enough. But I can tell you the result of it: in about twenty or thirty years, there were eleven cabins full of Jollys living all up and down through what we still call the Jolly Cove."

"Tell us the story about Phyleete," my brother or my cousins or I would beg Uncle Frank. This was my favorite of all the tales swapped between the two families.

"Phyleete Jolly," he began. "Well, actually nobody really knows how to spell 'Phyleete,' you just have to sorter have a phonetic guess at it. You see, the Jollys never figured a name was anything that would need to be written down. As long as a name was something you could holler at somebody to get his attention, that seemed like enough to them!

"Anyway, Phyleete was married to a woman whose given name was 'Wife.' He was the one who had given it to her. This name worked very well, because whenever he hollered for her, no matter where he was, there was never any confusion about who answered.

"I used to hear it said,"—Uncle Frank was really winding up now—"that if Phyleete and Wife Jolly had worked as hard in the daylight as they did in the dark they would have been rich folks. But they were poor. They did, however, have twelve children—eleven boys and one girl. Then they quit."

Uncle Frank began. "The daughter, she's the easiest one to start with. The daughter was so normal that you could meet her on any street in any city in the country, and you wouldn't even notice her. That's how normal she was. You know, we just don't pay much mind to people like that.

"But the boys: you wouldn't miss *them*. They were a little different. Most people said they were just a little bit subnatural.

"Why, when those boys started walking, it never occurred to them that whether you're looking down or not, the ground is going to be there. They thought they better have the ground in sight before they stepped on it. So they all walked, every one of them, with their eyes fixed on the next spot their foot was going to hit.

"Yes sir, all of 'em walked just staring right at the ground in front of them. You could recognize them way off, shoulders bent, looking down, walking always in a straight line (so only the one in front had to figure out which way they were going and the others could rest their minds until it was their turn to lead).

"People in Iron Duff said they had the ground memorized! Myrtle Medford said she had seen them play a game when they were little boys, blindfolding one another, leading the blindfolded one all around, then taking off the blindfold to see if he could tell where they were just by looking at the ground. Of course, she said, if they slipped and looked up, they were all lost!

"And their names…" Uncle Frank thought for a moment. "It was like this: Phyleete and Wife just couldn't think of names for those boys when they were born. I mean, all the names they could think of already belonged to someone. So they just didn't give their boys any names at all when they were born.

"As they got bigger, though, the people around in the community began to give them names based on outstanding things each of them did.

"For example, the oldest one, when he was walking around, every time his left foot hit the ground, his tongue would run out of his mouth. There he'd go, staring at the ground, tongue popping in and out like he was trying to catch a fly. Everybody started calling him 'Lizard,' and that became his name: Lizard Jolly."

Uncle Frank was on a roll now and we all listened, fascinated. He introduced us to more of the Jollys.

"One of the Jolly boys liked to go through the woods and pick up nuts to eat. Acorns, walnuts, hickory nuts, hazelnuts, he didn't care what kind they were. Only trouble was he always cracked them in his jaws. Why, in the fall of the year, his lips and tongue and chin would turn pure brown from cracking walnuts with his mouth! Working on those hard hickory nuts and walnuts built up his jaw muscles until his cheeks were almost as broad as his shoulders. They said that if he could get his head through a hole, the hole was big enough for his whole self to come through. And acorns, he just ate acorns like they were popcorn, hulls and all!

"You won't be surprised to learn that by the time he could reach the lower limbs on an oak tree, everybody was calling him 'Squirrel.' By the time he was a full-grown young man, he had outgrown that childhood name and by now and forever was called 'Jaws.'"

"Tell us about Rake, Uncle Frank," my brother asked.
"Oh, yes, Rake. Well, when he was a young man, this particular member of the Jolly brotherhood had a fine set of his own natural teeth. But one day, as he was walking down near the edge of the garden, he came to where Phyleete had left a particular garden tool in the tall grass. The implement in question was lying on its back with its teeth in the air when our soon-to-be-Rake stepped square on the teeth.

"As the laws of physics apply even to the subnatural, the handle of the garden implement rose rapidly into the air, and a combination of simple lever and fulcrum in action relieved the offender of his front teeth.

"He became an embarrassed young man after that. Toothless, he was filled with fear that strangers would ask, 'What happened to your teeth?' He decided that the best thing to do was to step right up to newcomers and tell them what had happened. So, he would approach strangers, stick out his hand for a shake, place his tongue in the gap to illustrate his loss, and explain: 'Rake!' People thought this friendly fellow was introducing himself, and they responded appropriately. Finally even he accepted the fact that he had been named 'Rake.'

"Then there was the brother who was scared of water. The story is that he got to be sixteen or seventeen years old, and because of his terrible fear, he had never had a bath. The whole community named him 'Rancid.'

"Well," Uncle Frank laughed. "We can't meet all of them at one time. I'd better tell you boys a little story about them."

"Wait!" I requested. "Tell about one more before that. Tell about the one that tried to walk on the fish pond."

Uncle Frank consented. "All of these Jolly boys, as we all know by now, were very careful about checking out the ground as they walked, but there was one who was once let down by the very ground he was looking right at.

"It was wintertime, and the fish pond was frozen over. It looked just like the ground to him, so he started across, taking a short-cut home, his eyes on every step.

"Well, the shortest way home took him close to where the creek from up in the cove comes into the back of the pond, and when he got there the ice was just too thin. He watched two steps in a row go right through the ice, and ended up standing in freezing pond water past his knees. It's a good thing the thin spot was right close to the bank!

"That poor boy never trusted the ground again. Whenever he was out and walking about, he would take every step twice: once to check the ground to be sure it was going to hold, and then a second time in the same place to put his whole weight down. It was slow moving from place to place the way he did it—right, right...left, left...right, right...left, left.

"Now, you remember that when these Jolly boys went out together, they always walked single file so everybody except the leader could rest his brain a little. They took turns at leading.

"The crisis came when this double-stepping brother had to take his turn in front. He slowed them down something awful. There they were, one behind the other, while up front he was leading them—right, right...left, left...and so forth, on and on.

"If they were traveling along a narrow trail where no one could pass, this double-step leadership could hold up the entire traveling public. Folks in a hurry would come up behind the slow-moving line and be unable to pass in the narrow trail. They would get impatient, then mad, and they'd finally holler, 'Whoever is in front, quit clogging up the trail—move on out and let us get past!'

"And so, distrusting of the very ground on which he walked, this double-stepping brother became known as 'Clogger,' and gradually, down through the years, everyone who moves around the way he did is called a 'clogger.' Why, sometimes they get to doing that double-stepping so rhythmically, they almost look like they're dancing!

"But on with the story. It was September. The sky was clear, and the moon was full. That big field of corn between the dairy barn and the fish pond was almost ready to cut. I had finished milking in the evening and was starting on back to the house just as that full moon was coming up through the trees on the east-side ridge behind the house from where I was walking.

"About the same time I saw the moon, I heard somebody talking. Sounded like they were way down in the cornfield and the only words I could make out were something like, 'C'mon, let's get outa here.' I just knew it was somebody stealing corn, so I sneaked down through the field to catch whoever it was. Got all the way to the bottom of the field and nobody was there, but I could still hear them talking on towards the fish pond.

"I eased through the chinquapin bushes in the dip below the corn field, and just as I climbed the bank of the dirt dam around the fish pond to where I could see into the road that cut across the dam from the barn to the cove pasture, I saw who it was!"

"Who was it?" I broke in.

"Well," he laughed, "it wasn't entirely anybody! lt was seven of those eleven subnatural Jolly boys, caught out there after sundown, trying to find their way home by the light of the moon. They were just a-muttering to one another: 'Let's git outa here...let's us git home...purty soon it'll be so dark we can't even be able to see how to talk...we'd better git on outa here...'

"Lizard was in the lead. The six who were with him were rowed up like little ducks behind their mama. They were all barefooted—hadn't been real cold weather yet—and Lizard was taking them all toward home.

"Suddenly disaster struck." Uncle Frank's face filled with foreboding. "I don't know if you know this, but in addition to Lizard's other physical peculiarities, his skin was too tight for his body. It was kind of like trying to put a hundred pounds of cow feed in a fifty-pound sack. Something had to give somewhere to compensate.

"With Lizard, it worked this way: every time his jaw dropped for his mouth to open, that tight skin pulled his eyes shut! Why, poor Lizard was going through life blind half the time! He never did see what his right foot was doing!

"On that particular night, he got, so to speak, blindsided. His big, bare left foot took a well-planned step, his mouth dropped open so his tongue could run out, the tight skin pulled his eyes shut, and his big, bare right foot came forward in the great darkness of Lizard's closed eyes and collided with inhuman force and matching indignity against a rock which was sticking right up in the middle of the road.

"The indignity instantly faded in the face of pain. Lizard's right big toenail had been knocked loose, and blood was streaming everywhere. He rolled on his back and wailed, surely on the edge of death.

"His brothers gathered around to try to help. 'Something must of hurt him,' Rake surmised.

"Jaws agreed. 'Yeah, I don't think he could holler like that unless something was a-hurtin'.'

"Rancid joined in. 'I know what it is...h'its *pain*. Mama says there ain't nothing hurts as much as pain! Lizard's got a pain and h'its a-hurtin'.'

"Slowly Lizard began to realize that his wound was not mortal, and slowly he began to realize that flat on his back (a position no male Jolly had ever assumed before), looking *up* at his brothers (a direction in which no ground-watching Jolly had ever even glanced before), he could see, high above the trees, a sight never before seen by the Iron Duff Jollys.

It was the September full moon, and Lizard, who had never looked up in his life, had no earthly idea what it was.

"I just stayed back in the chinquapin bushes and watched," said Uncle Frank. "Thought it might be interesting just to be quiet and look on for a while.

"As Lizard's pain subsided and he knew he wasn't going to die, it occurred to him that he should share his new discovery with his brothers. 'Look up!' he hollered. 'Look up in that big pine tree!'

"It took a moment for the concept 'up' to sink in, but when it did, the six other brothers all looked up, only to see what seemed for all the world to be a huge, round light hanging high up in a tall pine tree. They argued for a while both about what it was and about how it got up there.

"Then Rake had an idea. 'Let's poke it down,' he said, and finding the longest limb they could find, the Jolly boys poked loose needles, bark, and pinecones right and left, but the big light just wouldn't come down.

"Lizard was watching the whole thing thoughtfully. He finally rose from the ground and limped over to his brothers. 'That thing ain't gonna come loose,' he said. 'The limbs is too close together. But that's all right, boys; they's another one sunk in the fish pond!'

"They looked," Uncle Frank smiled, "and there it was! Another moon (though they didn't know that was what to call it) was shining right up out of the depths of the calm fish pond.

"'Let's fish it out,' said Lizard, and his brothers eagerly brought the long limb to the edge of the pond and began raking the water for all they were worth!

"It looked like they had it moving pretty well—as long as they kept raking the water. Whenever they stopped, that thing seemed like it settled right back to the bottom where it had been to start with. This just wasn't going to work.

"Then," Uncle Frank said, "Jaws got an idea. He was looking for a snack, and he spotted a great big old oak tree just full of acorns and with a huge, long limb that stretched out over the fish pond.

"'Climb up in that tree with me,' Jaws invited his brothers, 'and while I'm snacking, the rest of you-all can get out on that big limb and reach right down in the water and get that purty thing!'

"Well," said Uncle Frank, "it looked like a fine idea. The seven Jolly boys all climbed up in the oak tree, and while Squirrel was eating acorns, the rest of them got out over the water on the big limb.

"Lizard was still taking his turn at being the leader. He hooked his legs around the limb and dangled, head first, toward the water. The limb was much too high, and even when he stretched his arms downward, he couldn't come anywhere close to touching even the surface. But the sunken moon was in sight right under the limb, so they couldn't give up now!

"'One of you'uns get me by the feet and let me on down,' Lizard said to his brothers. Rake did as he was told. With his legs wrapped around the big limb, he got a firm grip on Lizard's ankles and lowered him toward the water. It was encouraging, but still not close enough.

"'Another'un hook on to ol' Rake,' ordered Lizard. 'We're a-gettin closer!'"

Uncle Frank delighted in describing the scene that was unfolding, and we all joined in the delight as we closed our eyes to picture it better in our minds.

"That still wasn't close enough, though, so they kept adding on to the chain, one brother after another, until in ten or fifteen minutes there was *six* of them hanging straight down from that limb, each holding the next by the feet like a little string of possums hanging on to one another by the tail. And Lizard could *almost* touch the water. And he could clearly see that whatever that thing in the water was, it was almost exactly straight below him!

"'One more,' says Lizard, 'one more, and I'll have it!'

"The only one who hadn't already joined the lineup was Jaws. He was still back in the tree munching acorns. It was his turn. He stuffed his cheeks full of acorns, came out on the limb, hooked his legs across it, and got hold of his brothers.

"It was quite a load, the six of them, and Jaws's hands were still a little messy from eating acorns. He thought to himself, 'I'd better spit on my hands and get a better grip.'

"Now Jaws was always a cautious and thoughtful young man, so he thought this all the way through before he did anything. First of all, he figured out he was going to have to be quick, so he got all ready to spit before he ever let loose. When he was all ready, he did everything as fast as he could. He let loose, spit on both hands, and grabbed. But in his great haste, all the muscles in his body had tightened and his legs had straightened up.

"And so, not knowing where he was leaving his brothers, Jaws fell straight down, *ker-splash*, into the fish pond. Being a caring boy, his first thought was of his brothers. He looked up toward the big tree limb to see if they were okay, and they were all gone! At this moment, Jaws had reached the outer edge of his reasoning power and he said, with astonishment, 'I don't see how they all fell—I just let loose of them for a second!!'

"Now all seven of those boys were in the fish pond. The moon was forgotten as a new panic took over: none of the Iron Duff Jollys had ever learned to swim.

"Anyway," Uncle Frank helped us to visualize the sad scene, "what I saw was the terrible and potentially tragic sight of seven nonswimming Jollys in the actual very act of drowning. They were going under, slapping the water with their arms, flailing with their legs, hollering, and blowing water ever which a way.

"Just as I was trying to figure out the best way to try to save the most of them at once, the day (or the night, that is) was saved. It was Rancid who did it. Being natured the way he was, Rancid hated being in that water. All that splashing around made it even worse—some of his best dirt was coming loose. So Rancid quit trying to swim and stood up. When he did, he discovered the water was only about three feet deep, and he was safe!

"Rancid bellowed to his brothers, 'Stop swimming, stop swimming! You'll drown clean dead! Stand up and let's walk out of here!'

"And so, leaving the moon in the fish pond forever (it was probably stomped to pieces by now anyway), the seven Jolly boys followed Rancid onto dry land.

"'Are we all here?' asked Lizard, thus raising a new problem. For since the Jollys knew that none of them could swim, it stood to reason some of them might have drowned before Rancid's great lifesaving discovery, and each was secretly afraid that if someone had drowned, he might be the one. 'If one of us goes home drowned, Mama will kill him!' Rancid lamented.

"Now boys," Uncle Frank was talking to us now. "I have failed to introduce you to the one Jolly boy who now had the best chance to verify the presence of the others. They called him 'Brains.'

"You see, all eleven of the Jolly boys could count…all the way up to ten…in order!…*if* it was daytime and they had their hands out in front of them. Brains discovered, all on his own, that he could count plumb to twenty if he looked at his feet when his shoes were off! Why, when he went to school barefoot, he felt like it was cheating on arithmetic. Sometimes on hard problems, he'd be counting up on toes two or three desks in front of him. When cold weather came and everybody had to wear shoes, old Brains almost failed arithmetic."

I thought Uncle Frank was wandering off the track. "What did Brains do to save his brothers?" I asked.

"Oh, *that*. Well, they knew that seven of them were supposed to be there, but when they said their names to check the roll, some of them couldn't remember if they were part of the seven they were looking for or not. So, Brains said, 'You'uns line up, and I'll count ever'body who's wet.'

"It was a wonderful idea. They lined up. Brains got off to the side and counted from right to left: 'One, two, three, four, five, six…One of us ain't here!' They all got upset.

"Lizard exerted his leadership. 'Come here and get in my place, Brains, and let me count back the other way.' The two of them switched places, Brains in line and Lizard off to one side. Lizard counted from left to right: 'One, two, three, four, five, six… He's right! One of us is drowned for sure!' This was very upsetting.

"All seven Jolly boys, the six just counted and Lizard himself, fell on the ground screaming and squalling. 'One of us is drowned, one of us is drowned, and it might be meee!' I was afraid," said Uncle Frank, "that if they hollered like that all night, my cows might not give any milk in the morning. It was time to take some action.

"I decided," Uncle Frank told us, "that it was time for me to save those seven Jolly boys from drowning!"

"What did you do?" we all asked. We had heard the story before, but we wanted to hear all of it again.

"I stepped right out of those chinquapin bushes and asked those hollering boys just what the trouble was. 'One of us is drowned,' screamed Lizard, 'and we don't know which one of us it is.' Then they proceeded to tell me the entire story just as if I hadn't been there to see it with my own eyes to begin with. They looked mighty desperate!

"'Well, boys,' I says, 'Line up here behind me and I'll see if I can figure out some way to see who's here and who's not. Lizard you get in front, Rake next, right on back in single file. Now follow me.'

"Then," Uncle Frank was explaining the plan to us now, "I led them all through a gap in the cow pasture fence and proceeded right up through the pasture, by the light of the moon, looking for something."

My brother couldn't wait to hear. "Were you gonna take a cow-pile census, Uncle Frank?" he asked.

"I'd rather call it a 'sun-cake census' boys. That sounds a lot nicer!"

"What's that?"

Uncle Frank explained. "First you look for a medium, well-done sun cake…that's one that's somewhere between being fresh baked by the cow and cooked hard as a rock by the sun."

"Pretty soon I spotted one which was just right—a little crust on top, but still nice and tender on the inside. 'Now, boys,' I says to the Jollys, 'Gather round this here sun cake. Lizard, you be first. Get down on your knees and whatever you do keep your tongue in your mouth. Take a big breath, then poke a hole in the crust of that sun cake with your nose.' He did it! I turned to Rake next. 'Rake, don't bother Lizard's signature—you sign in on your own.'

"One after another, each of those Jolly boys got down on their hands and knees and made their own nose mark in the crust of that sun cake. I could check their noses and tell instantly who had signed in and who was still holding out.

"When they were all signed in, I said to them: 'Now, boys, let's gather around here and all together, out loud, count the nose holes in this sun cake.' And so we counted: 'One, two, three, four, five, six, *seven!*'

"Lizard hollered, 'You did it, Mr. Davis! You saved us! None of us drowned! Hurray! Hurray! Hurray!'

"And boys," Uncle Frank looked straight at us, "the last thing I saw that night was those seven subnatural Jolly boys, happy as they could be, following Lizard home, and from time to time wiping a little sun-cake batter off of their noses!"

# Whatever Happened to the Jollys?

We always wondered whatever happened to the Phyleete Jolly family. They were nowhere to be found in Iron Duff and we had never been shown where they were buried, so it just seemed like the thing to do to ask Uncle Frank whatever became of this remarkable group.

The question was posed, and as usual, the answer which followed was a story in itself.

Uncle Frank told us the whole thing started when he was getting ready to leave home to go to work in Wilmington in the shipyard during the Second World War. The night before he was to depart, he was rechecking the clothes he had packed when there was a knock at the door.

There stood Phyleete Jolly.

Uncle Frank's first thought was that Phyleete had just dropped in to tell him goodbye before he left for his ship-building job. Phyleete, however, seemed unaware of what was happening in the world at large as he suddenly and loudly blurted out, "Mr. Davis, we've growed out of our house. We're going to haf to git us a bigger one!"

This announcement came as no surprise to Uncle Frank. After all, two adults, one natural daughter, and eleven subnatural sons living in a one-room log cabin would seem to be a too-full house in anybody's deck. He was amazed they had made it this far and wondered if only the fact that some of them forgot to go to bed each night made enough space for those who remembered to get a place to sleep. He thought things over, and then gave his reply to Phyleete.

"Why, Phyleete," Uncle Frank began, "it's about time you had a little more space to move around in."

"That would be all right, too, Mr. Davis," Phyleete said, "but right now we just need more space to live in. Why, I don't hardly know what moving around means no more."

"Let me just be as straight as I can with you, Phyleete." Uncle Frank thought that if he didn't pass on some quick, simple instructions, they could be standing out there on the porch all night.

"I know that you and the boys know how to build log buildings. Why, you've helped me build everything from the corn crib to the hen house. So, you just go on up there in the cove and pick out a good place, and then you and the boys just build you a bigger house. Make it high enough to at least have a loft you can sleep in."

Phyleete smiled broadly.

"I'm leaving in the morning," Uncle Frank went on, "to go build ships to help win the war. Mama will be staying here by herself, and the farm is going to be shut down for a while. You just go on and build your new house, and I'll come over and see you when I get on back from the war."

And so Uncle Frank left for Wilmington, the farm was shut down with Grandmother living in the house by herself, and Phyleete and his eleven subnatural boys began making plans to build their new house. They got right to work and were finished in no time.

With the farm not being worked, nobody ever wandered up into the Jolly Cove while Uncle Frank was gone. All the natural boys in Iron Duff had been drafted into the army, so there wasn't even anyone wandering around squirrel or rabbit hunting. And Grandmother had neither the time nor the inclination to monitor the Jollys.

Three years passed. Uncle Frank came home from the shipyard. He started checking around the farm, just surveying how things had fared since he had been gone and figuring what needed to be done to gear up operations again. He rode his Ford tractor up the farm road into Jolly Cove and became the first natural human being to see the Jollys' new house.

There was nothing unusual about the house. It was just a bigger rectangular log structure than the one they had lived in before. This one was, if not actually two stories high, at least high enough to have a good sleeping loft upstairs. No, the unusual thing was not the house, but where the house stood.

The Jollys had one particular problem with the location of their old house which they wanted to be sure to avoid this time. There had been a spring-head above what other people would have called the 'yard,' and in wet weather, the whole plot of ground in front of the house turned into a real bog.

Sometimes people were even known to get stuck in the yard trying to walk to or from the house. There they would stand, mired way above their knees. The Jollys would have to toss food out to them to keep them alive until the wet spell was over and they could get loose.

Clogger was very bad about getting stuck in the yard since he always gave the wet ground two chances to get him: his first step to check the ground would create a good-sized hole, and his second hit with the same foot would take him in up to his hips. Clogger had spent about half of every wet spring season stuck in the yard!

Phyleete had determined to build the new house on a spot where the front yard would always be firm. No more getting stuck! He had searched the cove for such a solid location, and when he found the perfect spot, he built the house there. Three years later, Uncle Frank was the first person to see that the Jollys had built their new house right smack in the middle of the road!

It was good, hard ground, and convenient, too. Just step out the door and you were on your way down the road. Come up the road and you would eventually be right in the house. They even had a back door so they could go on up the road as well as down it.

Uncle Frank stopped dead in his tracks when he saw the house. When he told Phyleete to pick a place and build a house, it never occurred to him that anything like this might happen. He just stood there and stared at the house, spread completely across the road—the very road which was the one and only access to the entire back half of the farm. There was not enough room for even a team of horses to pass now, let alone a wagon or a mowing machine.

Phyleete and Wife came to the door. "How do you like it, Mr. Davis? We're not just living now, we can even move around!"

"It's a very nice house, Phyleete. Its an *awful* nice house." Uncle Frank couldn't think of anything else to say.

He also couldn't go to sleep that night for trying to figure out what to do about the Jollys' house. Of course, he thought, he could build a new road around it, but that surely would be a job and would take a terribly long time.

The best (the only) thing to do was to get the Jollys to move the house.

They wouldn't have to take it apart. It was built smack on the ground with a dirt floor, so with the front and back bottom logs acting like sled runners, Uncle Frank figured the whole house could actually be scooted sideways far enough to get it out of the road without disturbing anything in it.

The real engineering challenge was to get the Jollys to move the house without knowing what they were doing or why they were doing it. He didn't want them to be embarrassed about having built it there in the first place.

Uncle Frank laid in bed a long time that night trying to solve this problem. Suddenly, about midnight, the solution hit him like a flash of lightning.

"I know what!" He sat right up in bed as he exclaimed out loud. "I'll give the Jollys a cow!"

Neither the simplicity nor the efficiency of this plan would be immediately obvious to anyone ignorant of the Jollys' past history with cows.

Uncle Frank had once before given the Jollys a cow, but they had lost her. A few years earlier, he had taken a wide, Jersey cow over to Phyleete's old house and said, "Here, Phyleete, I thought you could use a milk cow...well, she's yours!"

Phyleete took the rope from Uncle Frank and asked, "How do I keep up with her, Mr. Davis? I can't just stand and hold her all day. And how do I feed her?"

"That's no problem," Uncle Frank answered. "She'll just pasture around here on her own. There's plenty of grass all over the cove. But you need to get a cow bell to keep up with where she is. You go to town the first chance you get and buy you a cow bell at the store."

"Okay, Mr. Davis. Thank you for the cow!"

And so, the very next day, Phyleete headed for town to buy a bell for his new cow.

Uncle Frank was waiting out in the yard when Phyleete passed by on his way back home. He didn't seem to have a sack or anything, so Uncle Frank called him over.

"Phyleete, did you buy a bell for the cow?"

"I sure did, Mr. Davis!" He reached way down in his overalls pocket and pulled out a little round bell like you would put on a sheep or a goat.

"Why did you buy that thing instead of a *cow* bell, Phyleete?"

"Well, Mr. Davis, you should have heard those big old cow bells. They made an *awful* racket. Why those things were so loud you could put one on a cow, come out the door, hear it ringing, and the cow could be plumb over on the other side of the mountain. But put this here little bell on her, come out the door, hear it ringing, and she'll be right there!"

In the face of this kind of logic, what could Uncle Frank say? He watched while Phyleete put the little round bell around the cow's neck.

In less than a week, Phyleete reported that the cow had "got herself lost!"

All that had happened back before Uncle Frank had gone to the shipyard, and now as he remembered it, he formulated the perfect plan to use the gift of a new cow to get the Jollys to move their new house without their even knowing it!

Early the next morning, Uncle Frank picked out a good, heavy Holstein milker and a long piece of stout rope. He headed for the Jolly Cove.

He knocked at the door of the new Jolly residence until Phyleete, Wife, and a few of the boys came out all together to see who was there.

"I've brought you a housewarming present," Uncle Frank exclaimed as he held up the rope to the cow.

"It might be cold in there, Mr. Davis," Phyleete replied, "but we ain't sleeping with no cow to keep warm!"

"That's not what I mean," Uncle Frank tried to explain. "A housewarming present is just something you give somebody when they've got a new house. This is the first chance

I've had since I was gone to give you anything. This is a new *milk* cow for you Phyleete; she's not a sleeping cow."

"We lost the last one," Lizard put in.

"I remember that," said Uncle Frank. "That's why I've brought this long rope. We're going to tie this one to the house so she won't get lost.

"Now, Phyleete," he went on, "I've brought plenty of rope, because she needs all the room she can have to roam around and pick grass, so let's put a good, long rope on her. But…it can't be too long. You see, I'm going to plant corn in that big field just on the other side of the road there and I want to be sure that this cow won't be able to get in my corn field when it comes up. You help me figure out how to do this right, Phyleete."

So, Uncle Frank had Phyleete hold the cow right by the edge of the soon-to-be cornfield while he measured out just enough rope to reach from there to the house. The excess rope was cut off, and the cow was tied to the house with just enough slack to reach the edge of the cornfield but no further.

The next day, Uncle Frank plowed and harrowed the field and then he planted the corn.

The weather was just right, and in two weeks time, the corn was showing. That cow seemed to smell those tender blades about as soon as they were out of the ground. By the time the corn was ankle high, it was driving her crazy. She lost all interest in picking free grass.

In the mornings, Phyleete or one of the boys would give her a good scoop of dairy mash when they milked, but as soon as she had eaten that, she headed straight for the corn.

Of course, she couldn't reach it. The rope was too short. Uncle Frank had very carefully seen to that. But there the poor cow would stand, pulling at the end of her rope, bellowing all day at the corn like it might come to her.

All the Jollys got a big kick out of this. They would lean back and laugh and laugh while they watched their cow trying to reach the corn.

"You ought to see that cow you gave us, Mr. Davis. She ain't got good sense. Why, she thinks that if she jerks and bellers long enough, she'll be able to reach her a bite of that new corn."

Uncle Frank laughed too...and he waited.

When the corn got to be about knee-high, Uncle Frank slipped up to the Jollys' house one night when the moon was dark. Very quietly he took the rope off the cow and untied the other end of it from the house.

Then he replaced it with another rope which was about four feet longer than the first one. He took the old rope with him and went home to bed.

The next morning, the Jollys were up bright and early as always. They all piled out the front door into the road and checked the weather by looking at the ground to see whether the sun was shining on it or rain was bouncing off it. It was sunny. Then they noticed that they didn't hear their cow bellowing, and they followed the outstretched rope to check on her.

There she was, to their amazement, four feet into the cornfield. She wasn't bellowing because she was busy eating corn to beat all. She had almost cleared the good arc of a circle which, at its middle, reached nearly four feet into the cornfield.

Uncle Frank was hiding in some bushes across the road, and he watched all the Jollys came outside to help figure out what happened.

They just couldn't believe it. They *knew* that cow wasn't supposed to be in the corn.

Finally Lizard offered the solution: "I know what happened, boys. I can tell you just *exactly* what happened. She jerked and pulled on that rope 'til she moved the house. We'll have to put it back! We can't just leave her standing there in Mr. Davis's corn field."

And so, with Wife watching the cow to tell them when to stop, Phyleete and all eleven boys put their backs against the end of that log house and pushed with all their main strength until the cow was back out of the corn where she was supposed to be.

By that standard of bovine measurement, they were all convinced the house was also back where it was supposed to be. Uncle Frank could see, however, that the house, pushed four feet from where it was built, was now almost half-way out of the road.

"One more piece of rope," he hold us later, "and I figured the road would be clear."

So Uncle Frank waited another month while the nibbled-off corn made a good start at a comeback. Then he eased back up to the Jollys' house and by the dark of the moon, added another four-foot extension to the rope.

He was up in the cove bright and early the next morning so he could watch the Jollys make their discovery.

As soon as the sun was high enough for the sunshine through the window of their cabin to hit the dirt floor inside, the Jollys saw it was time to get up.

Uncle Frank watched the door open. Lizard was out first, followed by his brothers. He looked down the rope for the cow, and there she was, munching those new blades right back off of that corn again!

"Look!" Lizard pointed. "She done it again! She done and moved the house again in the night, and we didn't even feel it! We're going to have to push it back to where it's supposed to be!"

Uncle Frank had to hold his hat over his mouth to quiet down his own laughter! He hid right there in the bushes and watched while Phyleete called Wife out to watch where the cow was and he and the eleven brothers put their backs to the end of the house. With a great clamor of grunting and groaning, they pushed the house another four feet.

It was wonderful! The Jollys' house was now completely out of the road, and they, by their carefully employed scientific standard of bovine measurement, were sure that it stood exactly where it had been built.

Uncle Frank felt good. The road was clear. The Jollys were none the wiser, and he had provided them with a good section of clean grass floor each time the cabin had been moved.

Now, any normal person should have been satisfied with that. But Uncle Frank got to thinking...

"How far...how far...do you reckon those Jollys would actually move that house four feet at a time?"

And so he would water that little spot in the cornfield and side-dress it with nitrate of soda until it sprouted some good, new growth, then he would sneak, in the dark of the moon, and add a few more feet of rope to the growing distance between the Jollys' house and their cow.

Sometimes he would hide and watch the result, and sometimes he stayed in bed and noticed later that the house indeed had moved again.

Gradually, as summer progressed, the Jollys' entire house was moving...four feet at a time...right up through the Jolly Cove, and they didn't even know it.

As fall weather began to come in, the house was getting on up on the mountain to where there was a pretty good tilt to it. This actually helped the Jollys in a way, because, all sleeping on the straw in the cold loft, the slope made them sort of roll together. They did keep a lot warmer that way.

Only two of the eleven boys ever noticed anything unusual at all.

The first to notice was Shovellip. This one and only Jolly with a three-syllable name was *not* the person you would want to have in line in front of you at a buffet dinner!

He would pile his plate with several layers of food, put his chin on the table and his lip under the edge of the plate, then he would take a fork in one hand and a spoon in the other and *shovel!*

Shovellip noticed that if he sat on one certain side of the table, all he had to do was give that food a little nudge and it would just about walk right into his mouth on its own. But if he sat on the opposite side of the table, he had to work himself to death shoveling with both hands just to get a mouthful. In spite of this observation, however, he still failed to realize that it was because the table (and the house) were on a thirty-degree slope.

One other brother made an interesting observation. He was one half (or maybe a little less) of the one set of twins the Jollys had.

I knew the twins were called "Picker" and "Likker" long before I knew how or why they got their names. I assumed that Likker probably had a drinking problem and that Picker was some kind of a string musician.

When I mentioned this guess to Uncle Frank, he laughed and then straightened me out on both of them. *"Picker,"* he said, "never played any kind of instrument except his nose, and *Licker,"* (not "Likker" at all) "got his name from having a tongue so long it would reach the bottom of a milk glass."

"Licker was the one," Uncle Frank went on, "who washed all the dishes. When Phyleete noticed this boy's proclivity for plate cleaning, he came down one day and asked me for a handful of short roofing nails. I gave them to him before I ever knew what he wanted them for."

I didn't understand. "What does this have to do with Licker Jolly?" I asked.

"Well, just listen a minute," Uncle Frank said. "Next time I went up to their house, I realized that Phyleete had taken the tin plates they ate out of and had nailed them right to the table! After every meal, Licker would go around the table and clean all the plates. After that, everything was already set for the next meal!"

"Did he really do that?" I could hardly believe it.

"Why sure," Uncle Frank assured me. "Phyleete told me it saved on food quite a bit. He said if somebody visiting happened to eat with them and then saw Licker wash the dishes, they never did come back for another visit. Imagine how much extra food that saved!"

With the house (and of course, the table) now at a thirty-degree angle, Licker noticed that a strange thing happened as he worked around the table washing the dishes. When he was licking from the same side that Shovellip liked to eat from, it seemed like he hardly had to bend over at all for his tongue to get to the plates. But when he got around to that side where it was so hard for Shovellip to eat, he got right dizzy and once or twice he actually fell on the table while he was doing his clean-up job.

Still, by the scientifically applied standard of bovine measurement, the Jollys were quite certain that their house remained where it had been since they had built it!

"Uncle Frank," I had to ask, "how long did this go on?"

"Well," he chuckled, "when we cut the corn in the fall, we left that end of the field standing for what you might call 'cow bait,' or maybe it was 'Jolly bait.' I kept on adding rope, until by Thanksgiving, the Jollys' entire house was perfectly balanced on the ridge of the Kansada Mountain, and that poor cow, that cow was at the end of a rope three-quarters of a mile long, still jerking and bellowing at that ripened corn!

"The only comment Phyleete was ever heard to make was this: 'It sure seems like you can see a lot farther down from the house when the leaves are off the trees.'

"Why, since they didn't have a clock," Uncle Frank added, "they didn't even realize that it was taking longer and longer to go to milk!"

"Did you stop there?" I asked.

"Oh, yes. We had to. Any farther and the Jollys would have slid down the other side into Jonathans' Creek."

"Is that the end of the story?" my brother asked.

"No, son. We've just now got them set up there on the mountains. We still have to get 'em down."

"How long did they stay up there?" It was my turn to ask.

"All winter long...and up into the spring of the year."

We listened carefully because we knew something was about to happen. "Then... It was the weekend of Easter, if I remember things right. Our whole family was gathered down at the farm to spend the weekend with Mama.

"It was Saturday night, and we had already finished supper and were just visiting when a great sudden storm came up.

"First the wind started blowing, then we heard thunder crashing and saw lightning, and before you knew it, there was as hard a downpour of rain as I have ever seen. It was really some spring storm.

"We had gathered at the living room window to watch the lightning, when all of a sudden brother Harry spotted something funny up in the Jolly Cove."

"What was it?" my brother asked.

"Be quiet and he'll tell us." I was terribly anxious to hear this out.

"It looked for all the world like a lantern light. We all looked at it, and then I reminded everybody all about the Jollys moving their house, and said it was probably one of them out in the storm for some reason, carrying a lantern.

"Harry laughed and said that one of them might be going to milk, 'cause the way they always looked down, they might not realize it was raining!

"We watched as the lantern came on down through the cove and kept going. The light passed by above the fish pond, then on down through the bottom and out of sight around the bend toward the Medfords'.

"We did talk a little about hoping they were all right, but we thought that if they needed help, they would have come straight on to our house. The wandering lantern just remained a mystery as we all went to bed for the night.

"The next morning, the storm was over and the sun came up bright and clear.

"While we were eating breakfast, we heard a cow right outside the kitchen window in the yard. We all went to the window, and there was the Jollys' big Holstein milker in *our* yard with her rope frayed through and dragging on the ground behind her.

"'Something's not right,' sister Mary said, and every one of us started out walking toward the Jolly Cove to see what had happened in the storm the night before to wear the cow's rope through and let her escape.

"When we got up to the Jollys' house, we saw what was wrong. The Jollys' house wasn't there.

"It was not too hard to figure out what had happened.

"During that great and terrible storm the night before, the Jollys' house had slipped loose from its perch there high on the ridge of the Kansada, and it had started sliding right back down the path made by the very same house itself as the Jollys pushed it up to its winter location.

"Water had surely built up behind it until it began to float—we could see where it stopped scraping on the ground.

"Why, boys, the light we had seen the night before had *not* been someone out in the storm with a lantern...no...that had been the actual light in the window of the Jollys' entire *house!*

"At some point, the cow's rope parted and she was set free. The house, though, had gone on.

"We had watched it (without even knowing it) sail across the fish pond, over the low dam, down through the flooded Flat Field, and disappear around the bend in the flooded creek on its way past the Medfords' house."

"Where did it go?" My brother couldn't stand it any longer, and I was glad he had asked.

"We searched everywhere," Uncle Frank went on. "All the way to the Tennessee River. Then we realized what had happened.

"Once that house got to floating, it just kept going, with all the Jollys asleep in the loft and no one to stop it. It had floated right off our land and into the Pigeon River, down to Cataloochee Creek, on to the Little Tennessee then the Tennessee, the Ohio, the Mississippi, and maybe even all the way to the Gulf of Mexico. Boys, the Jollys just washed away!"

"Where'd they end up, Uncle Frank?" we both asked.

"Well, boys, for a long time I wasn't sure myself. Then, you remember that trip Kathleen and I took out to Springfield, Missouri, to see Frances after she was married?

"We got to the other side of Tennessee and saw the Mississippi River for the first time. I drove off the main highway and down into a little Tennessee town there beside the river just to get a closer look at it. And do you know what?

"Out there beside the river, I saw six grown men and women, all walking in a straight line, looking right at the ground with their tongues popping in and out!

"Then I knew."

I knew what had happened. As the Jollys' house had washed away on that long ago Easter morning, they had awakened one at a time, realized the peril they were in, and one at a time, jumped off to dry land, spreading the entire subnatural Jolly line way out, all the way down the Tennessee, Ohio, and Mississippi River valleys.

"Once they got established, of course, they began doing what they did best!"

"*Proliferating!*" my brother answered, though I knew he didn't know what the word meant.

"That's right, son," Uncle Frank said, "Proliferating east and west, until now, boys, do you know what happened to the subnatural Jollys?"

"What?" we both cried.

"They're *everywhere!*"

# Jolly Old Saint Nicholas

The last-born of the Jolly brothers was one who was called "Tracker" by all of his Iron Duff neighbors Though last of the boys in order of birth, Tracker was actually named before many of the others because he had a talent so outstanding that it drew attention to him as soon as he could crawl.

He had a photographic memory for the ground.

You simply could not lose this youngest Jolly. He could remember the most minute detail of the ground, right down to particular blades of grass and grains of sand. The neighbors who observed this remarkable ability named him "Tracker" before he was even old enough to walk.

If Tracker had been one of the seven brothers who fell in the fish pond, the group would never have gotten lost to begin with. Later on, when Uncle Frank took him places in the Jeep or the car, he would ride with his head hanging out the window so he could watch the road passing by underneath and tell where they were going.

It was no fun having him along for a ride in the wintertime. He insisted on sticking his head out the window, and so he froze everyone else in the car half to death.

At each holiday season a great portion of the family gathered at Uncle Frank's house because this was, after all, the home place of the Iron Duff Davises. Over the years all the small cousins were visited by Santa Claus while they were at Uncle Frank's house for Christmas. They never saw him, of course, but no matter how far from home they were, St. Nicholas always brought their presents.

One year, Uncle Frank got an idea. "Why don't I make arrangements," he thought to himself, "to have old Santa Claus himself show up and deliver the presents on Christmas morning?"

When he shared his plan with my daddy, Daddy wanted to know just how he was going to manage that.

"It's simple," Uncle Frank answered. "They've got a Santa Claus suit up at Belks store. I'm going to borrow it over Christmas and dress up for the little ones."

"Aw, Frank," Daddy objected, "they'll know it's you, and that won't be any fun!"

Uncle Frank knew that was probably true, but he didn't want to give up on the idea.

He decided to hire Tracker Jolly to wear the suit and be Santa Claus and bring presents to all the little Davis children on Christmas morning.

And so the plan was made. Uncle Frank borrowed the Santa Claus suit from Belks store a few days before Christmas and took it, along with all the cousins', nieces', and nephews' presents, to the Jollys' house. The project was now in Tracker's hands.

Christmas Eve arrived. Tracker was excited. He loaded all the presents in the big sack early in the afternoon, even though he wasn't to appear at Uncle Frank's house until breakfast time the next morning. He put the Santa Claus suit on and took it off a half-dozen times.

His only concern was the weight of the sack of toys. With all those children at Uncle Frank's for Christmas, Tracker was given an extra heavy load.

"I've got an idee!" he said to his brothers. "Why don't I take all the toys down to Mr. Davis' barn, and take the suit there, too? I can make two or three loads if they are too heavy. Then tonight I'll spend the night in the barn, and in the morning I'll put the suit on there and be real close to the house for one stout haul. The best I can remember it's only a hundred and forty-six rocks, three cow piles, six thousand and thirty blades of dead grass, three rotten planks and eleven thousand and one grains of sand from the barn to the house!" (Tracker truly did have a topographic memory.)

"Why, that's a real good idee," his brothers chorused.

Tracker and his brothers made several trips to Uncle Frank's barn before dark to get everything set up for his playing the perfect role of Santa Claus, carrying all the toys to the house in one load the next morning. Tracker slept on the hay in the barn, dreaming of what a nice Christmas this would be.

The next morning, Tracker got up, put on the Santa Claus suit, put all the toys in the one, big sack, slung it over his shoulder, and opened the barn door to get on with his mission.

To his horror, the world looked like a Christmas card. The ground was completely covered with a soft blanket of snow and Tracker, unable to see the ground, had no idea which way to go to get to Uncle Frank's house.

He would have been able to see the house if he had only looked up, but since he had never done such a thing in his life, he couldn't really be expected to start now—especially not with that heavy load of toys on his back.

For a few moments he panicked. "I'm lost! I'm lost!" he thought. Then he did look at the floor back inside the barn door and at least remembered that he was starting out in the barn.

Finally Tracker made a decision. He would wander, directionless, out into the snow in hopes that he would either see something sticking up from the ground that would help him or meet someone who could direct him to Uncle Frank's house. He did try kicking the snow aside for a few steps, but even he could see that would take so long Christmas would be gone before he got out of the barnyard.

And so Tracker started out on his frustrating journey across the unknown land of snow. He wandered right past Uncle Frank's house, right through the yard, but since he didn't look up and since he couldn't see the ground, he didn't know where he was.

He wandered across the bottom field and right up through the Jolly Cove quite near his own home, but he didn't know where he was. He wandered in a big circle around the fish pond and back toward Uncle Frank's barn where he had gotten lost to begin with.

Tracker began to despair. "There's nobody out here. Everybody's staying in the house and waiting for me and I don't know how to get there unless one of them comes out to help and nobody's coming."

Then, miraculously, he came upon a set of tracks in the snow. "Oh! Oh!" Tracker shouted. "I am saved! I am found! I will just foller these tracks until I catch up with whoever I'm following, and I know it will be someone who will help me get to Mr. Davis's house."

With new resolve, Tracker began following, in hearty pursuit of help, his own tracks!

For the second time, he passed through Uncle Frank's yard. For the second time, he crossed the bottom and trudged up into the cove. For the second time, he passed his own house, and for the second time, as he turned back towards the barn, he began to despair.

"Whoever I'm follering is a-walking too fast. I cain't catch him, not with this big load I'm a-carrying!" He was about ready to give up.

And then, suddenly, there were *two* sets of tracks!

"Oh, look!" Tracker exclaimed to himself. "Two of them! I'm a-follering two of them." He speeded up his pace, figuring that with two people to follow he had twice as many chances to get help.

This new burst of hope drove him on until it seemed like no time until he was following *three* people, and then it was *four!*

Around and around he went, as Christmas morning came and went, following his own round-and-round tracks. He was sure he was finally in the main road to somewhere because everybody seemed to be going this same way.

No one knows how long this might have gone on had not, by great good fortune, the sun come out in the afternoon and begun to melt the snow. At last Tracker came to a place where the snow was gone and he could see the ground. He saw that he was right in Uncle Frank's front yard, and kicking the last few feet of snow aside, he found his way to the steps and approached the front door of the house.

Uncle Frank was exhausted. All day long he had been promising the children that Santa Claus was coming, and he was fast running out of excuses about why he had not yet arrived. It was a time of real comfort and joy when a knock came and Uncle Frank opened the door to see Tracker—who had probably walked close to twenty miles by now, carrying that sack of presents every step of the way.

"Look children!" Uncle Frank almost wept. "I told you he was coming—it's jolly old Saint Nicholas!" The day was saved.

Uncle Frank was afraid to ask Tracker what had happened; he wasn't sure he was up to hearing the explanation. He did get a clue when Tracker asked him later in the day,

"Mr. Davis, did about fifteen or twenty people come by here a little while ago?"

When Uncle Frank said no, Tracker concluded the matter.

"Then I'm glad I quit follering them when I did, or there's no telling where I might have ended up!"

And as for all Uncle Frank's little nieces and nephews? They were happy for Santa Claus to go back to delivering presents in the night the way he always had.

# Uncle Frank Invents the Electron Microphone

*I*t was the first Sunday in November, two days before election day.

Election Day was important to Uncle Frank. He was always running for something. This year, Uncle Frank was once again a Democrat candidate standing for reelection to the Board of County Commissioners.

Since this was the last weekend before the election on the coming Tuesday, Uncle Frank was busy with last-minute campaigning. He executed this election-eve politicking by sitting in the sun in his front yard not bothering anybody.

"I figure," he said, "that at this point the best way I can get votes is just not to annoy anybody. Everybody knows who I am, and I reckon that some people will vote for me over some of those other fellers just by me being quiet for a day or two!"

So, there we sat—Uncle Frank, my brother, our daddy, and a few cousins—taking in the sun on a beautiful, clear, late autumn afternoon.

"If anybody wants to know any more about this election now," Uncle Frank mused, "they can just come down *here* and *ask* me. I'm tired of telling people stuff."

About that time, we all heard a car coming down the road. Everybody looked to see who was coming. On a Sunday afternoon, it was probably Aunt Mary or Aunt Esther.

When it came into view where the gravel road curved out of the woods, we saw that the vehicle we'd heard was not a car at all, but an old, rusty, '38 Ford pickup truck with the front fenders held on with baling wire.

The rear fenders and original truck bed were long gone and had been replaced by a flat, homemade bed of rough boards. The front fenders flapped and the board truck bed danced as the old heap bounced toward us in a great cloud of dust.

Uncle Frank recognized the truck as belonging to a family of Rathertons who lived towards Crabtree. Daddy knew them, too.

"Look there, Frank," Daddy laughed. "You've got your wish. Some of the Ratherton boys have come over here to talk politics with you!"

"Don't joke about the Rathertons, Joe," Uncle Frank said. "They're all Democrats and they all vote, whether they get paid for it or not. There's enough Rathertons to either put a feller in office or keep him out!

"You don't upset the Rathertons. Whatever these two want, let's keep them happy so the whole bunch of them will vote for me. I'd be surprised if they want to talk politics though. After all, this bunch lives downstream from the Jollys."

The old Ford pickup rattled to a stop. No one inside moved until the cloud of dust which had followed the truck down the road drifted past the cab and the air cleared. Then the doors opened, and two of the Rathertons stepped out.

They were two big, overgrown boys who could have been anywhere from fourteen to seventeen years old, and except for one's being heavier than the other, the two looked very commonly the same.

Both had sharp, peaked noses and prominent Adam's apples, which bobbed up and down with every step. Both wore caps, and when they removed them as they approached, it was easy to see that both, even at this young age, had thinning hair on their cap-shaded heads above reddish, sunburned faces.

Neither had ever shaved, and both had sprouts of hair of various lengths around and about their faces.

They tried to walk in step with one another, but the heavier one's shorter legs kept him falling behind, and every few steps he had to skip once or twice to keep up.

The two Ratherton boys were dressed for squirrel hunting, with .22 rifles leaning against their shoulders. Each one had a tow sack to carry his anticipated kill home in.

The brothers approached Uncle Frank.

"Hello, Mr. Davis." The thin one spoke for both of them. "We're Rathertons. My name's Weasel, and this here is my brother Awful."

(Uncle Frank remembered my Daddy coming home some years before after one of his public-record information-gathering trips for Granddaddy to report that Mr. Ratherton had told his wife, "I wanted a boy awful bad." His wife, to please him, consented, and so 'Awful' became the baby's name. 'Weasel,' on the other hand, was a fairly common name in the Crabtree-Iron Duff area.)

"Hello, boys," Uncle Frank replied, very kindly. "What can I do for you? It surely is a nice day, isn't it?"

"Sure is," Weasel answered. "Ain't it, Awful?" he prompted his brother to agree.

"What can I do for you boys?" Uncle Frank asked.

"We's wanting to go squirrel huntin', and daddy said if we was to ask you, you would let us—'cause we're such good Democrats."

That was so!

We all knew right then that Uncle Frank was in a bind. There was talk all over the countryside that the squirrels were not as plentiful as usual, and he wanted to preserve the population on his farm for his own family. If he were to let anybody else hunt on the farm, it would surely be the Jollys since they lived there.

Here he had two Rathertons, blatantly and politically representing all their Democrat relatives, wanting to make a two-sack haul on Uncle Frank's already scarce supply of family squirrels.

We all wondered what he would do.

"Well, boys," he replied at last, "I have just one rule about hunting on my farm."

("Here it comes," my brother whispered. "He's going to turn them down.")

"That rule is: you have to eat what you shoot. You boys are going to do that aren't you? You're not wanting to shoot up my squirrels just for the fun of it?"

"Oh, no, Mr. Davis," Awful licked his lips as he answered. "We're going to eat every squirrel we can shoot. Me and Weasel will skin 'em and clean 'em and Mama will fry 'em and make a little squirrel gravy." He was rubbing his tummy now in anticipation. "There ain't nothing as good as fried squirrel and gravy and cathead biscuits!"

Uncle Frank seemed satisfied. The boys were hunting for food. Still, we couldn't believe that was all he was going to ask of them before sending them out to commit mass squirrel murder!

"Have a good time, boys—and good luck! You just hunt all up through the Jolly Cove there and wherever you want to, and don't forget to vote for me on Tuesday."

"We always do that, all of us!" Weasel assured him.

We watched in amazement as the Democrat Rathertons headed toward the Jolly Cove to get paid (it seemed to me) for the votes which Uncle Frank had just bought from them with squirrels.

They had gone about ten steps when he called out to them. "Hey, boys…wait just a minute…there's something I forgot to warn you about." Weasel and Awful turned back, but Uncle Frank met them halfway to explain his neglected concern.

"Look up there on the mountain, boys." He pointed up to the ridge above the Jolly Cove. "Do you see that little white building up there?"

We all knew that he was indicating the World Headquarters Building of the Greater Iron Duff Fox Hunters' Association. The Rathertons nodded. Not being among the Iron Duff fox hunters, they didn't know what they were looking at.

"Take a good look at that little white building, boys. I don't know how I could have forgotten to tell you about it—why, that's about all that's been on my mind lately." We all looked on incredulously as we listened. We didn't know Uncle Frank had been thinking about anything but the election.

He continued his instruction to the Ratherton brothers. "As I said before, boys, you feel free to hunt all you like, but I think it would be a good idea *not* to fire a rifle within about fifty yards or so of that white building. It's on account of the noise."

None of us, beginning with the Rathertons, had any earthly idea what he was talking about.

"Now go on, get going with your hunting."

Weasel and Awful made a slow start toward the cove, pointing up to the ridge of the mountain where the World Headquarters Building was and talking with one another.

Uncle Frank let them go about twenty steps this time before he called out again.

"Boys, boys, boys!" He was trotting to catch up with them as he called them to a stop. "Now that I think about it," (he was talking so all of us could hear him), "maybe fifty yards isn't enough, *if* that building's in sight. Don't fire, boys, no matter how far away you are, if you can still see the place. That's it: out of sight, fifty yards...in sight, don't shoot! It's just on account of sensitivity to noise, boys, and it's important to our history.

"Now go on...get on up there! And have a good time!"

My brother and I were as confused as the Rathertons. We looked at Daddy. He just gave us a smile and a shrug which seemed to say, "I don't know either, but your Uncle Frank usually knows what he's doing."

The Rathertons seemed stuck. They just stood there looking at Uncle Frank. Then they looked at one another. Then they looked up at the World Headquarters Building. Finally they huddled together and spent a good few minutes talking. At last they broke huddle and approached Uncle Frank. Weasel did the talking.

"Mr. Davis," he began. "Me and Awful just don't know what to do. We do want to get us a mess of squirrels awful bad, but we just don't know what's going on up there where you're a-pointing. Awful's scared you're going to try to scare us, and we ain't going to vote for you if you scare us. I told him I was just going to tell you you've got to explain to us what's going on."

Uncle Frank looked very serious.

"Come on here and sit down, boys," he said to the Ratherton brothers. "I had hoped that you would just catch on, but since you didn't, and to be sure that all of your family votes for me on Tuesday, I will just tell you the entire and whole story—if you can keep a secret."

We all gathered around. Even Daddy was determined not to miss a word of what Uncle Frank was about to say.

"Now, boys," he began, "this is highly classified information. I'll have to swear you all to absolute secrecy."

"We can keep a secret," Awful said.

"Then unload your guns and get ready to swear," he instructed. "You can't trust swearing that's done by somebody holding a loaded gun! Everybody knows that."

The boys both unloaded, then stood, serious and straight, in front of Uncle Frank. He turned to Daddy, my brother, and me. "If you're going to listen, I'll have to swear you, too! Now, line up with Awful and Weasel."

We all lined up.

"Cross your heart and spit on the ground; hope to die if you breathe one word. Now raise your right hand. *Do all of you swear on the sacred history of Iron Duff that you will not reveal one word of what you hear on this day?*"

"I swear!" we all, even Daddy, pledged in unison.

"Then it's time for you to hear the whole story." We sat down under the maple tree. Uncle Frank pulled up a wooden chair, and the great secret began to unfold.

"You may remember two or three years ago when those government map-checkers came through here. Three fellers from Washington, nice as could be, camped up in the cove for about two weeks.

"They had all kinds of scientific instruments with them. They were checking the accuracy of government maps. Said there were teams of them doing it all over the country. They were checking slopes and elevations and measuring water and drilling in rocks and every sort of thing."

Awful broke in. "I don't get it, Mr. Davis. Were they measuring squirrels too?"

"No," Uncle Frank chuckled. "Just the shape of the land.

"One day they came down here to the house all real excited. Said they thought they had discovered something wonderful, but they needed me to help them check it out. Said they needed somebody with a voice pitched like a native.

"Well, I went on up there with them, and they had me doing the funniest thing you ever saw. They had me standing at different places and just hollering. Seemed like most of the places they asked me to holler made a real good echo. Sometimes the sound bounced back and forth three or four times before it died down.

"Now this is what I'm leading up to, boys. That's exactly what those scientists were looking for.

"They had discovered on their own that when they were talking in the Jolly Cove, they could always hear one another, even if they were talking real soft and were a long way apart. That's when they developed the theory. They just had me hollering to check it out!"

"What theory?" I asked before the Ratherton boys had a chance.

"I'll tell you," he said. "Those government scientists, with all of their complicated instruments had calculated that the entire Jolly Cove is a *helexically semi-hemispherical doubly reticulated decibel-enhancing Newtonianly conceived and Heisenbergianly perfected natural geological echo chamber!*

"Now you know boys! What do you think about that?"

The Ratherton brothers just sat there. My brother and I just sat there. Even Daddy just sat there. Finally Daddy broke the silence. "I believe you're going to have to tell them, Frank. I'm not sure much thinking's going on."

"Well," Uncle Frank finally said, "The existence of the Jolly Cove as the previously described perfect echo chamber means that every sound ever made in there from the dawn of creation to this very moment is *still in there,* just echoing back and forth, getting softer and softer and softer, even though most of those sounds haven't been heard in hundreds, maybe thousands of years! Don't you realize what that means?"

We sat still, afraid to move, but the Ratherton boys both shook their heads.

"Can you imagine it, boys? Everything that has ever been said in the Jolly Cove...still echoing around up in there!"

Finally Weasel spoke up. "What good's that going to do, Mr. Davis, if you can't hear any of it?"

"Now, boys," Uncle Frank responded quickly, "I realize that you've got to hold several things in your mind at once to comprehend all of this, but try. This, Weasel, is where the government scientists come back into the picture."

He looked at all of us, then focused down on Awful and Weasel.

"Tell me, boys," he asked, "did you boys ever go to school?"

"Course we did, Mr. Davis," Weasel answered. "I got through the sixth grade for the second time before I quit when I was sixteen, and Awful's already in the fifth grade and he's only thirteen. Why, he's come through two grades in three years. He's smart!"

Uncle Frank already knew who he was dealing with, but this seemed to confirm it. He went on. "Well, boys, in school did you ever hear about an electron microscope?"

"I know what a microscope is, Mr. Davis!" Awful was excited. "You can see all kinds of little boogers through it. We had one in the fourth grade."

"That's just a plain, old microscope, Awful. An electron microscope is one you have to plug in! Why, it can blow little things up so much you can breathe under it and whoever's looking through can actually *see* what your breath smells like. They can tell what you had to eat two days before just by looking at your breath under that microscope. That electron microscope can help you see things that are fifteen-thousand times too little for human beings to look at!"

Weasel made the connection. "I'm catching on, Mr. Davis. You've got one of them things up there *looking* for them echoes!"

"Not quite, Weasel; you don't *look* for echoes, you *listen* for them. But you are about to catch on. Now listen…" He looked at all of us intently as he talked.

"This is top secret boys, but I'm going to tell it to you because you have spit and sworn not to tell anybody. Those government scientists up in Washington, D.C., have now invented an *electron microphone!* That thing can do for hearing what the electron microscope does for seeing. It's a wonderful breakthrough for spying!

"Now, boys, I'm about to pull all this stuff together for you," he said.

Daddy muttered, "It's about time." It all sounded pretty important to me.

"Boys,"—Uncle Frank was intense—"we got a special grant from the Daughters of the American Revolution and bought one of those electron microphones. That thing is set up right up there in the Jolly Cove, and it is picking up all those faded sounds made from the first day of creation until right now.

"It's feeding everything it hears into a big tape recorder that has a tape eighteen inches wide to hold it all. That's what's in that little white building you can see up there.

"About once week, we send the tape to Washington, where they play it through an *institutional grade spectrophonic voice separator,* and out of the other end of that machine come clear conversations spoken hundreds of years ago."

We all just listened and stared. I didn't want to miss a word of this.

"We're rewriting the history books, boys! Why, did you know that some of the first Jollys who lived up there had fought in the Revolutionary War? One of them actually knew General Washington himself. After they moved here, they spent the rest of their lives reliving those old war memories.

"Boys, now we've got on tape actual first-hand conversations about the Revolutionary War. And the grandchildren of that first bunch of Jollys were Confederates. We've got enough about the Civil War already for a new book. Why, history has been kept alive up in there!"

Uncle Frank turned to my Daddy, like he needed a special dose of his own. "Joe," he said, "the Bureau of Indian Affairs is interested in the tapes of sounds made before the first Jollys ever moseyed in up there. They want to find out more about the Cherokee people. You know, we do find arrowheads up in there every once in a while."

I was really picking up on the importance of all this now, and I added what seemed to me to be the natural conclusion. "And the sounds of creation, Uncle Frank, way back when the earth was cooling off? I'll bet some scientists would love to have those. Maybe we can find out what dinosaurs sounded like!"

"You're a smart boy," he said to me.

Now it was time to turn back to the Rathertons. Uncle Frank spoke to them. "Weasel, you and Awful know it all now. So, go on up in there and get you a good mess of squirrels. You know exactly how to be careful and what to watch out for! Good luck, boys!"

With that, the Ratherton boys started for the Jolly Cove.

About fifty yards later, they stopped. They were talking and then they seemed to be arguing. There was a lot of pointing and arm waving, but we couldn't make out exactly what they were saying.

Finally, they came back to where we were standing.

Again, Weasel was the speaker. "Mr. Davis, we shore do appreciate you letting us hunt here, and we *really* appreciate you filling us in on what's going on up in there. But we've thought about it, and we wouldn't want to mess up the course of history by making a big noise in the wrong place, so we believe we'll go on back up and see if we can't hunt above Guy Chambers's place.

"We'll tell you one thing, though: everybody in our family is going to vote for you on Tuesday. Why, if you can get a hold of stuff that's already been over and done with for two hundred years…law, we reckon you can surely take care of the present time way better than anybody else could!"

And so Uncle Frank's quick invention of the electron microphone saved the squirrels *and* the election.

# Uncle Frank Learns to Speak Polish

*A*s long as I could remember, there had been a little frame
house situated on a low hill just beyond Uncle Frank's
dairy barn. When the house was built, or by whom or what
its original purpose was, I never knew.

It was always called "the tenant house," and though as
a child I never knew what a "tenant farmer" was, I did know
that the house was sometimes empty and sometimes oc-
cupied by various families whose members seemed to be
helpful to Uncle Frank, especially with milking and feeding
around the dairy.

At the close of the Second World War, the house happened to be standing empty when Uncle Frank read in the
news about Eastern European refugees and discovered that
many of the people he was learning about were homeless
immigrants in need of a place to make a start.

The tenant house was offered for this purpose through
the Red Cross, and in a short time, a young couple from
Poland arrived as new residents of the farm at Iron Duff.

They were the first foreigners, except for the tourists
from Florida, that we had ever seen!

"DPs" my daddy called them, explaining that this meant "displaced persons," and telling me a little more about the war than I wanted to know.

I never knew the Polish couple's name. Whatever it was, it had been deemed unpronounceable by the Iron Duff tongue, and in a theological effort to address then both personally and properly, Uncle Frank simply renamed them "Adam and Eve." They accepted the new names with amazing grace and were so known to us all.

It never occurred to us that, being unable to speak a word of English when they arrived, Adam and Eve were more lost with us than we were with them. Still, their adjustment was remarkable, and in a short time, we could actually communicate quite well with one another.

Uncle Frank summed it up: "Adam is brilliant and Eve is a pure genius. Why, they are not only learning to speak English, but they have *already* taught *me* to speak Polish so that I can communicate with them in their own language. It is a difficult but remarkably beautiful language!"

Uncle Frank's neighbors were amazed! One of their own, in less than a month's time, was conversing fluently with two people from *Poland* in their own native tongue.

I had heard Uncle Frank tell about this before I heard firsthand proof of it, but I was still impressed beyond words when I heard my first actual conversation.

We were sitting in the kitchen at Uncle Frank's house when Adam came to the back door. He knocked, and then called through the screen door, "Daviski! Daviski!"

Uncle Frank was on his feet and on his way to the door when he answered Adam, "Oh chee-whilli, chee-whilli!"

My attention was absolutely riveted!

Adam uttered a long, unintelligible sentence. I thought I heard the word "cow," or at least something that sounded like that, somewhere in the middle of it. Again it ended with his calling Uncle Frank "Daviski."

Uncle Frank's reply was as intelligible to me as Adam's utterance had been. I looked at my Daddy and said, "Listen. He can really do it. Uncle Frank can really speak Polish!"

"Aw, son," Daddy said, "that's just a lot of gibberish."

"Gibberish?" I replied. I had heard of English and Spanish and Polish, but never of Gibberish. "What is *Gibberish?* Is Gibberish a special dialect of Polish they are speaking?"

He never answered me, or if he did, I was so fascinated listening to the foreign conversation that I did not hear his answer.

On Saturdays, Uncle Frank would take Adam and Eve to town when he went to do his week's shopping and visiting. All up and down Main Street, people were amazed as he translated for them.

"Daviski?" Eve would ask Uncle Frank, then ask what sounded to us from the tone of voice like it could be a question.

"Oh chee-whilli, chee-whilli!" he would quickly answer. People would ask him, "What were you talking about?" and he would fill them in on the entire Polish conversation. It was amazing how much they could say in Polish with so few words being exchanged.

"Eve was asking me what time it is," he'd say. "She's getting hungry." Or, "Adam wanted to know where to find the bathroom—I told him how to get to the one on the first floor at the Courthouse."

On the way home, they would often stop at Charlie's Drive-In to get something to eat. The regular customers at Charlie's were always amazed to hear Uncle Frank translate the menu from English into Polish.

He would pick it up and read aloud, "Oh chee-whilli, chee-whilli!" Adam and Eve would both silently nod their heads. Uncle Frank would then turn to Charlie and order for them. "They both want a fried-egg sandwich and a cup of coffee. And now that I think about it, I think I'll have the same!"

Even Charlie, who had seen absolutely everything and had heard even more than that, was amazed.

One day they stopped by our house on the way back to Iron Duff. I met the three of them at Uncle Frank's car. Uncle Frank got out of the car, turned back to Adam and Eve, and spoke to them in Polish. "Oh chee-whilli, chee whilli!" he said.

"I told them I'd be back out in just a minute," he reported. "I believe they are just going to wait in the car."

"Uncle Frank," I began. The question had been growing in my mind for some time now. "Why is it that when *you* talk in Polish, it always sounds like you're saying the same thing over and over again? I mean, when Adam and Eve talk, I can't understand them, but everything they say sounds *different.* Every time you say something in Polish, it's just the same old 'chilly-willy'–sounding stuff over and over."

"Well, son," he answered seriously, "you have to realize that my Polish vocabulary is much more limited than theirs. And on top of that, you have to know that slight changes in inflection and emphasis can make words that seem to sound the same to the untrained ear take on very different meanings to those who are articulate. You'll just have to listen more carefully. You'll catch on!"

It sounded reasonable to me, but I did hear my daddy mutter something else about gibberish when he heard that explanation.

I am never quite sure just how long Adam and Eve stayed on at Uncle Frank's, living in the tenant house. Eventually, however, they did move on, either to join more of their family elsewhere or because they had a vision of greater fortune on their own.

Uncle Frank never forgot how to speak Polish, and though my daddy persisted in calling it "Gibberish," later events proved that, whatever the particular dialect was, knowing an obscure foreign language could be useful even if no one else in the vicinity could converse with you.

One such event happened a couple of years later on a weekend when our family was visiting at Uncle Frank's house.

It was Saturday. We were all still seated around the kitchen table after lunch. Uncle Frank didn't really have any heavy work to do until afternoon milking, so we all looked forward to a time of family talk and visiting. Suddenly we heard a car crunching its way down the gravel road toward the house.

My mother was seated next to the window, so she was the first to see it come into view. It was a long, shiny black Pontiac with two men riding in the front seat.

"Oh law," she uttered in dismay. "It's those Bible salesmen. They stopped at our house last week, and before I could get rid of them, I had learned the books of the Old Testament and fed both of them supper. If they get in here this early in the day, the whole rest of the afternoon will be ruined."

"Let's hide," I offered.

"That won't do any good," she said. "They've already seen the cars in the yard. They won't give up 'til somebody lets then in."

Uncle Frank had been watching and listening. Finally he offered, "The rest of you stay here and be quiet. I'll take care of this and be back in just a minute."

As Uncle Frank went toward the living room, he closed the kitchen door behind him.

The rest of us watched out the window as the black Pontiac came to a halt beside our car in the yard. The front doors opened and out stepped two of the fanciest men we had ever seen in our lives. They both had slicked-down black hair, parted in the middle. One had a pencil-line moustache.

The one who seemed to be the leader opened the back door of the Pontiac and took out a suitcase. He handed it to the younger one and then reached in and picked up a Bible it took both hands to carry!

We watched and Mother shook her head as they came toward the house. "That's them," she said. "We'll be stuck here for the rest of the day."

They came up the steps and onto the porch. We couldn't see them now, but we heard the sound as one of them knocked loudly on the screen door. Impatient, they knocked again. We heard Uncle Frank shuffling around loudly in the living room as he made his way to the door. We heard the door open.

One of the Bible salesmen said, "Good afternoon, sir. Are you the master of this abode?"

"Oh chee-whilli, chee-whilli!" Uncle Frank answered. My daddy could hardly keep from laughing out loud, but none of us made a sound!

A second voice asked, "Are you the one who lives here, or is there somebody else at home?

"Oh chee-whilli, chee-whilli! Chee-whilli, chee-whilli!" Uncle Frank happily answered.

There was a moment of silence. Then Uncle Frank offered, without even being asked, "Daviski, chee-whilli, chee-whilli?"

After a long silence, we heard one of them speak. This time he was not talking to Uncle Frank, but was addressing his partner. "I don't know," he said, "if this feller's a foreigner or just a damned idiot!"

"Don't matter," the boss answered him. "Either way he ain't going to spring for no Bibles. Let's quit wasting our time and get out of here."

As we saw them heading back toward the Pontiac we again heard Uncle Frank calling after them, "Daviski! Chee-whilli, chee-whilli?" It was too late, however, for the Pontiac was by now leaving in a cloud of Iron Duff/Polish dust!

As Uncle Frank returned to the kitchen, I said to my daddy, "See, Daddy, he *can* speak Polish, and even if it's not very good Polish, it got rid of those Bible salesmen a lot quicker than *you* could have in plain old English!" He had nothing more to say about that.

As time passed, Uncle Frank retained his mastery of Polish and even added other languages. In time he told us he could even speak Russian and that he had taught Russian to my Uncle Gudger so they could talk about *certain things* and not be overheard.

When my brother and I heard them together, we had quite a treat. Uncle Frank would call Uncle Gudger "Gudgerov" and unwind long sentences in Russian. Uncle Gudger would respond in kind. It still sounded pretty "chilly-willy" to me, but after the day with the Bible salesmen, I wasn't ever going to question Uncle Frank's linguistic ability again.

Uncle Frank told us once about how speaking Russian had saved him and Uncle Gudger one day.

A new highway to Tennessee was being built alongside the Pigeon River, and part of the building involved blasting and drilling two long tunnels through the mountains there. Uncle Frank and Uncle Gudger wanted to inspect them, but since it was a blasting zone, no one was allowed anywhere near the construction site at any time.

One Sunday afternoon, however, the two of them decided that no one would be working on Sunday, and this would be the perfect time to check out the mysterious construction project.

They got in Uncle Frank's truck and drove down the Pigeon River road to explore. They got to a fence which was covered with "Keep Out" signs, but with a little work, they took the fence down enough to get the truck through and kept driving to see what no one else had seen.

Finally, they rounded a curve at the tunnel site only to find the entire construction crew was there and at work. The project had fallen behind schedule, and they were working seven days a week. As soon as Uncle Frank's truck appeared, the superintendent, as mad as could be, came running over to see who in the world this was and *what* they thought they were doing

"What did you do?" It was Daddy who asked the question before any of the rest of us had a chance.

"I turned to Gudger and said, 'Oh chee-whilli, chee-whilli, Gudgerov!' and Gudger nodded his head to show that he understood. And then we talked a little more in Russian until that construction man quit hollering and started listening to us.

"Then I turned to the construction man and said, 'I apologize to you, sir, for our intrusion. We did not realize that you would be laboring on a Sunday. I am from the State Department, and this is Colonel Gudgerov, a Russian engineer.

"'We have made a deal at the State Department to exchange engineering secrets with the Russians, and I was to secretly show Colonel Gudgerov this tunnel. But we shall be going so that you may proceed with your work.'"

"Then what happened?" Daddy asked.

"They wouldn't let us leave!" he answered.

"You were in trouble, weren't you?" I asked.

"No, we weren't in trouble. They wanted to show us the whole thing. Why, boys, Colonel Gudgerov and I got a personal tour of the entire tunnel and an explanation of exactly how they did everything. Of course, I had to keep translating it into Russian for Gudger.

"One of them kept muttering to the others, 'That's the first damned Russian I've ever seen!'"

Daddy had heard enough of this foreign language stuff by now. He turned to me and said, "Son, when you go to college, don't you ever ask me if you ought to learn a foreign language. You get in there and learn every foreign language you can. If you haven't learned one other thing from your Uncle Frank, at least you will always know how important *that* is."

# Uncle Frank and the Crown Feed Boys

*U*ncle Frank was a strong believer in the value of education. That is why when he wasn't running for County Commissioner, he was often found running for the School Board.

That belief in education may also account for why he worked so hard at educating both his relatives and his friends whenever the opportunity arose.

It was another weekend in the fall of the year. All the hay was cut, baled, and in the barn loft. All of the corn was chopped and blown as silage into the two tall upright concrete silos. Enough firewood was chopped and stacked for reasonably foreseeable bad weather. The leaves were down, and the yard had been raked for the last time. Canning and freezing were long since done with.

The major work of the season was finished, and there was a scattering of beautiful, clear autumn days when the wind was calm and the low sun still pushed the temperature up into the sixties.

It was on such an afternoon that Uncle Frank had time to give me a few lessons in the more practical aspects of life.

"Never throw a rock at a hornets' nest," was his first lesson. "Those things are fast, and they've got some kind of radar to help them find who's annoying them. They'll get you!

"If you want to fight with stinging things, go for wasps. They're slow—and dumb. Why, you can take a rolled-up newspaper or a good handful of big weeds and eliminate a full generation of wasps in thirty seconds."

The second lesson of the day was in how to stomp a mud puddle dry. Uncle Frank demonstrated: jump with both feet right in the middle, then jump again every time the water tries to run back into the puddle until it is finally dry. (He did warn me my mother might not appreciate my learning this, but it was a *very* important thing to know.)

Now, in midafternoon, we were on lesson number three, on the importance of making up your own cuss words.

"Every once in a while," Uncle Frank began the lesson, "everybody needs to cuss a little bit. Not often, mind you. But once in a while, it is essential to be able to administer a good dose of profanity.

"Now, son," he went on, "the problem is that the need to cuss usually comes just at the time and place where you can't do it without either being embarrassed or getting into trouble. You see, at a time like that, if you use the same old ordinary cuss words that everyone else uses, everybody will know exactly what you're saying. Most of the time that just won't do.

"The perfect solution,"—I was catching on to where he was headed with this idea by now—"is to make up your own unique set of personal cuss words so that you can say *exactly* what you feel whenever you feel it, and no one will ever be the wiser."

He then shared with me some of his own private vocabulary and had me work at developing mine.

"Turkey britches!" I said, and then told Uncle Frank the term meant "the state of being covered by any form of animal waste."

He had me practice the new term and the apply it in several of its variants. I complied.

"Turkey britches on you!" I said, then, "You're full of turkey britches," and finally, "How would you like to be buried head first in a warm pile of turkey britches?"

He approved. "Now you're catching on! See? With your *own* cuss words you can be safely profane when and where you need to. Try a few more."

I went on to expand my secret profane vocabulary to include such nouns as "cinnamon toast," "chicken livers," and "Windex," and completed my lessons with phrases like "stain the grass," "take a bath," and "feed the cows." (He told me that he didn't want to know all the meanings of my words because they were supposed to be secret to me, and the only important thing was that I know what I was saying.)

After that, we stomped a few more puddles dry, knocked out another wasp nest, and secretly commented on it all with our own personal vocabularies.

We were having so much fun we didn't even see a big truck coming down the road until we heard the engine. When we looked up, it was almost right there in the yard.

I had seen machinery like this before, but not up close. It was a huge feed-mixing truck, set up to mix sorghum and other supplements in with one's silage. It looked like it would suck the silage in through one big pipe, mix it up, and blow it back out another.

Uncle Frank looked at the truck. I looked at Uncle Frank. I had seen him get rid of unwanted salesmen in a variety of creative ways, so I looked forward to seeing how he would dispose of these. Maybe he was going to speak Polish again, or maybe Russian this time!

Two young men got down out of the big truck. They couldn't have been on the job very long, as they barely looked old enough, even to me, to be out of high school.

As they approached us, Uncle Frank said to me in a low voice, "Son, are you in any big hurry to get home this afternoon, or could you stick around for a little entertainment?"

I had no idea what he had in mind, but I said, "I don't have a thing to do. Why, I can stay all afternoon if you need me to."

"We'll see," he nodded, and then the two of us looked up to greet our visitors.

"Hello," said the first one of the two feed-mixers. "Are you Mr. Frank Davis? We were referred to your farm by some of your neighbors. Then we saw that nice sign you have up at the end of your road."

Uncle Frank extended his hand and *in English*, admitted that he was, indeed, the very one they were looking for. I waited to see what kind of plan he must have in mind.

The first feed-mixer continued. "I am Mr. Rogers of the Crown Feed and Supplement Company. This is my associate, Mr. Reeves."

"Pleased to meet you," Uncle Frank said. "I don't think I've ever seen a contraption like this up close. Tell me what you boys do with it."

That was just what the Crown Feed boys were hoping for.

They started pulling out folders, then diagrams, then charts, then actual booklets, until they had assembled a display on the front lawn that could win a ribbon at the county fair!

The more they explained, the more questions Uncle Frank asked. Soon an hour had passed, and the lawn display now included implements, tools, and apparatus of every kind.

The second hour passed. I had never heard Uncle Frank ask so many questions, and the Crown Feed boys had never (in all their two weeks of experience, we discovered) had a customer so interested in understanding every detail of their enterprise. Why, it was going to take them a good half-hour just to load everything back up once this afternoon was all over!

Finally the sales pitch began to unfold. Uncle Frank was as enthusiastic about this part as about all the rest. Once he had all of his new questions answered, and another hour had passed, he spoke directly to the Crown Feed boys.

"Mr. Rogers," he began, "and Mr. Reeves, you have offered to me exactly what I have been looking for for my dairy cows. I am convinced that your 'Plan D,' the full-service sorghum-with-vitamin-and-mineral-trace-element formula, mixed with my already superior silage, will keep me in the butterfat lead in Iron Duff milk production. I have only one request as we begin to formally do business with one another," he said.

"Of course, Mr. Davis, how can we accommodate you?" Mr. Rogers asked while Mr. Reeves smiled like a satisfied cat.

"I want to see this contraption in operation a little bit before I sign the contract. No problem with that is there?" Uncle Frank asked.

The Crown Feed boys looked at one another. Mr. Rogers answered, "That is very much out of the ordinary, Mr. Davis. You see, if we ran some of your silage through the mixer to show you how it works, we would be, in effect, supplementing your feed supply before you have signed a contract for us to do so. If you backed out after that, Mr. Davis, there would be no way we could account for that activity on our inventory report." Mr. Reeves nodded in silent agreement.

"Oh, boys," Uncle Frank fairly begged, "I know this is what I want. *You* even know this is exactly what I need. I just want to be sure that big machine will actually work before I sign on the dotted line."

Mr. Rogers and Mr. Reeves entered into an extended confab with one another. Finally they seemed to agree on *something,* and they approached Uncle Frank.

"It is very irregular, Mr. Davis," Mr. Rogers said. "In fact, it is simply against the rules. But...since we all *know* that you *are* going to sign the contract, we'll do it! We'll run for five minutes and that's all!" Mr. Reeves nodded in agreement.

Slowly the Crown Feed boys backed the big feed-mixing truck toward the twin silos. All their presentation materials were left scattered over Uncle Frank's front yard, to be retrieved after the contract was signed.

We watched while the two of them swung a tube with a big screw inside it down from the side of the truck. This was inserted into the silage at the bottom of the upright silo and the big screw, like Archimedes' water pump, moved the silage from silo to truck.

We could not see what was happening inside the truck, but after a noisy grumbling sound, the now-treated silage was blown back into the top of the silo by way of a long pipe with a curved deflector at the top end.

Uncle Frank walked around, looked curious, and smiled while the Crown Feed boys allowed this apparatus to run for exactly five minutes. Then they shut it down, and all the sound died away.

"That's an amazing piece of machinery," Uncle Frank complimented. "Why, that is a perfect example of the finest way in which modern science and traditional farming go hand in hand."

The Crown Feed boys smiled. It had taken nearly four hours, but they knew they had made a sale!

I could hardly believe it! I thought Uncle Frank had been putting Mr. Rogers and Mr. Reeves on all afternoon, and here it looked like he was about to buy the whole thing, lock, stock, and barrel!

"You've got me sold, boys. Get the contract ready. Sign me up all the way for 'Plan D'."

The big truck was still hooked up to the silo, and the "scientific proof" was still spread all over the yard, but there was no time to gather that up now. Clean-up would have to wait until later. It was contract time now.

The Crown Feed boys climbed into the cab of the truck, started digging printed forms and carbon paper out of the truck's glove box, and before long had assembled a full, four-page contract for 'Plan D.'

They handed it, carbons in place for the purchaser's copy, to Uncle Frank, along with a pen for his signature.

He took the contract, looked at it, turned it upside down, looked at it again, then spoke to Mr. Rogers and Mr. Reeves.

"Boys," he began deliberately, "I know that the two of you are feed-mixing professionals, but you will understand if I tell you that my own father taught me that I should never sign anything without reading it first. You do understand that, don't you?"

Mr. Rogers answered. "Of course we do, Mr. Davis. Best way to do business is to eliminate problems before they ever start. You just read that right on through before you sign it."

The afternoon had already been long, and the sun was beginning to sink toward the Kansada Mountain, when Uncle Frank replied, "Well, *men*,"—even I noticed that he didn't call them "boys" this time—it was getting serious— "that's a problem."

I thought maybe he needed his reading glasses, but when he invited Mr. Rogers and Mr. Reeves to sit on an old bench beside the barn while he explained himself, I knew it was more than that. I knew a story was coming!

"Men," he began gravely, "when I was born, there were already seven children in the house, and every one of them was already older than I was. I was born into a family of four big brothers and three big sisters who already knew how to eat before I ever started to learn.

"Every morning started out the same old way. All the big ones could get up faster than I could, and they would get down to the kitchen and eat all they wanted before I could get out of bed. I just hated getting up so much, especially on cold mornings. By the time I got to the kitchen, I was lucky to get a little cold biscuit or a cornbread crust.

"It wasn't so bad when I was real little. Mama would feel sorry for me, and by the middle of the morning, she'd fix me a little something else to eat so I wouldn't whine around the house all day. The real awful time came when I got old enough to go to school.

"That first day of school was terrible! I got up so late that all my brothers and sisters had already eaten up every last bite of food before I ever hit the kitchen. Why, you couldn't even *smell* food anymore, it was so bare. I had to start out for school without one bite of breakfast in my belly.

"I like to have not lived through the day. My stomach hollered and my head hurt and I didn't think I was going to live to get home—it was a four mile walk back then, you know."

The Crown Feed boys nodded their heads. They had both heard about how far it was to school back in the old days.

"To make things worse, on the way home we had to pass by the sawmill. You men probably saw those old piles of sawdust back up by the road as you came down? Well, those sawmill women were already cooking supper and it not four o'clock in the afternoon! It smelled so good—chicken frying and turnip greens cooking—my little stomach like to have kicked over at the smell.

"At suppertime, Mama did at last fend for me, and she saved my life!

"The next day started out exactly the same way. I was the last one up, as usual, and we started out for school with the rest of them full and me on empty. But today I had a plan!

"I had noticed the day before that the sawmill yard was just full of children of all sizes—most of them looked just about alike—and not a one of them ever went to school. When we got up close to the sawmill that morning, I could smell the coffee and ham and eggs and biscuits and grits and fried apples, and I made my move."

Mr Rogers and Mr. Reeves listened with rapt attention.

"I just dropped out of line, watched my big brothers and sisters disappear out of sight as they walked on toward school, and I fell into playing with those sawmill children. A few minutes in the dirt and sawdust, and I looked just like the rest of them.

"Pretty soon they rang the bell for breakfast, and I just got in there in the trough with the rest of them and ate and ate and ate and ate until I had to sleep for about two hours to digest it all.

"At dinner time, I did it again. Then I played in the dirt with the rest of them until I saw my brothers and sisters headed home from school. When they came by, I fell in with them and went right home like I was supposed to.

"As soon as we were home, my brother Harry told on me!"

The feed boys laughed! "I'll bet you got your britches burned then," Mr. Rogers said, tickled, as he saw the picture in his head.

"No, men." Uncle Frank was serious. "That's not what happened at all.

"No, Daddy listened to Harry, then he lined up all seven of them. He looked straight at them every one and said, 'Whatever you do in life, children, don't be a tattletale. Keep to your own business and let other people take care of theirs!'

"Then he warmed all of *their* britches! Why there was so much crying and hollering going on that he plumb forgot to spank me!

"The next day was easy. I just took my own good time getting up. Of course, when I got downstairs, all the food was gone—but this day I didn't care!

"I followed the rest of them toward school until we got up there to the sawmill. I turned off from the road and fell right in there with those sawmill children the way I had the day before.

"All day long I played in the dirt and ate. There were already so many of those sawmill children there that they didn't notice an extra one—or if they did, they all thought I belonged to someone else.

"That afternoon, I fell back in line with my brothers and sisters and followed along back home. This time, nobody said a word about what had happened."

The Crown Feed boys looked like they couldn't quite figure out what this was all about, but they were suspicious of something.

Mr. Rogers asked the question. "What happened after that, Mr. Davis?"

"That's what I'm trying to tell you, men.

"What happened next is that I did exactly the same thing the next day and the next day and the next until I was sixteen years old, when sister Mary finally broke down and told Daddy that I hadn't never been to school. By then, boys, it was too late to start.

"I am trying, men, to tell you as gently as I can that *I can't read!*

"Now, boys,"—suddenly they weren't men any-more—"I want to sign that contract, but I can't *read* it, so I can't sign it. Don't worry, though, boys. My wife, Kathleen, reads for me. If you'll come on to the house, she can read it to me and then I can sign it. Just come on, boys."

There was an audible mixture of moaning and groaning as Mr. Rogers and Mr. Reeves fell in with Uncle Frank and headed for the house.

Suddenly Uncle Frank paused. "Of course," he said, "she's not home right now. But you're welcome to wait until she gets home. She's just gone to see her sister, and she'll probably be back in a little while. She went down there on Tuesday, I think it was, or maybe it was Monday... no, now that I think about it, I believe she went down there before the weekend...but she could be back in a little while. Course, it could be tomorrow, or she might decide to stay down there until Saturday or maybe Sunday, but you boys are *welcome* to wait 'til she gets back. She's the only one I trust to read this thing to me. You do understand that, don't you?"

This was too much for the Crown Feed boys.

It was also the moment when I came to know the importance of having your own set of cuss words. Mr. Rogers and Mr. Reeves just seemed to know the same old cuss words everybody else knew.

Uncle Frank and I listened, and *understood,* exactly what they said while they unhooked the feed truck, exactly what Mr. Rogers called Mr. Reeves, exactly what they said while they cleaned up the charts and signs and booklets and tools in the yard, exactly what Mr. Reeves called Mr. Rogers, exactly what they said about their jobs with the Crown Feed Company, and exactly what they said about Uncle Frank and his silos!

In fact, they cussed the sun down; they cussed until it was pure, pitch dark; they cussed all the way out of earshot as the big feed-mixing truck rumbled up the road and out of sight, never to return again.

And Uncle Frank and I laughed even longer than they cussed.

# Uncle Frank Cleans Up the Post Office

*S*on, don't ever be afraid of getting caught!"
This was one of Uncle Frank's cardinal points of wisdom and advice.

"Some people are so afraid of getting caught and embarrassed that they won't even begin to do the first half of what it takes to make life worth living. You can't buy adventure with shyness, son."

I wasn't exactly sure what all of this meant, so I asked my daddy. He told me that if I would ask Uncle Frank about what he did to clean up the Springfield, Missouri, Post Office, the story I heard would be, in itself, the very answer to the question I was asking. It turned out to be exactly that.

Being a dairy farmer, Uncle Frank was accustomed to getting up at four o'clock in the morning for the early milking. On those scattered occasions when he was away from home overnight, this early rising habit usually meant that he was up and wide awake long before anyone else stopped snoring.

He used these early mornings in strange places for exploration, and often discovered things on his sunrise walks which even the people who had lived in such places all their lives had failed to notice.

Some time after my cousin Frances got married and moved to Springfield, Missouri, Uncle Frank and Aunt Kathleen made the long trip to Missouri to visit with her in her new home. Uncle Frank was, of course, awake every morning long before anyone else was.

The first morning, he really did try to go back to sleep, but after that day, he just got on up and began to explore Springfield, walking for a good two hours before returning to the house for breakfast. Each day he headed out in a different direction, and in three days, never retracing his steps, he had covered most of a three-mile radius to the north, east, and south. The only direction left to explore was west.

On that fourth morning, Uncle Frank headed west. While his other walks had taken him mostly through quiet, residential areas, today he was aimed for the business district. Things looked much more alive there than they had along the quite streets where people lived.

Just as he was ready to circle a block and begin his return on the next street over, Uncle Frank noticed a lot of commotion and traffic. It was the United States Post Office, a huge brick building. The mail carriers and collectors in their host of little trucks and vans marked "Mail" were heading out to start their routes.

Uncle Frank watched a few of the carriers drive past, and then he turned to look at the big, brick Post Office. It was a mess!

First of all, the entire building was absolutely frosted with pigeon droppings. The nasty birds were everywhere. Maybe nobody could do anything about the pigeons, but what Uncle Frank saw that *could* be remedied was the trash. The street and sidewalk were littered with cigarette butts, smashed paper cups, cast-off candy wrappers, and discarded sale circulars. There were soft-drink bottles and old beer cans in the bushes in the front. And the parking lot! Why, the parking lot even had mashed-down cardboard boxes and second-hand diapers among its decorative treasures.

It was a pure-out urban mess!

Uncle Frank stood and watched for a few minutes while mail vehicles disappeared behind the Post Office building and others appeared with their loads for delivery. He stood and watched while early patrons stepped over and around refuse in order to pick up their mail. He stood and watched, noting that there wasn't a trash can in sight, while a postal patron on his way into the building tossed an empty paper coffee cup into the bushes.

Uncle Frank decided it was time to do something about this!

He walked in the front door, but he realized it was only seven o'clock in the morning and the customer service window wouldn't be open until eight-thirty. Then he remembered the advice he had often given to other people, and he muttered softly to himself, "You can't buy adventure with shyness, and don't be afraid of getting caught!"

He marched back out and followed the mail-delivery vehicles to the side of the building. The loading dock doors were open, of course.

Without a moment's hesitation, Uncle Frank walked up the four steps to the loading dock and pushed open the big double doors. He let them swing free behind him as he entered the mail-sorting area of the Post Office.

The sound of his dramatic entry caused a momentary lull in the noise as each worker glanced up and looked around. In that silent moment, Uncle Frank called out, "Gather up over here, all of you. Stop what you're doing. All of you listen to me!"

"Are you all here?" he asked as an assembly of men and women curiously drifted into the space around him. "Is the postmaster here?" An older, balding man nodded.

Uncle Frank addressed his gathered audience: "Get up close here...I want to be sure all of you can clearly understand me." It was dead silent in the Post Office as they listened intently.

"I am not, I *am not* going to tell you who I am, because if I did, a lot of you, especially the postmaster here, would be *terribly* embarrassed! But I will tell you this: I have personally observed the *deplorable* external condition of this public postal facility, and unless this place is *totally and completely* cleaned up by nine o'clock this morning, the whole lot of you are going to be looking for new jobs!"

With that he turned, left the postal workers standing there with their mouths hanging open, and walked out the same door he had entered.

As soon as Uncle Frank was out of sight around the corner of the building, he crossed the street and located a good hidden lookout spot behind a bush in a big yard. From there, he watched as the big show began.

He told us later he was sure that every postal workers' contract in Springfield, Missouri, was violated that morning and that the mail was also late in being put up and delivered— because every single person in that Post Office turned into an instant janitor.

They poured out the back door with leaf bags and trash cans, and filled with the righteous fear of their unidentified (but surely important) visitor, they started picking up trash right and left.

In less than thirty minutes, they had accumulated a load it took two garbage trucks to haul away.

Uncle Frank made a safe getaway, and no one complained about the mail being late. In fact, most people didn't even notice. Instead they were filled with amazement at how absolutely clean and nice everything looked all around the old Post Office.

# Uncle Frank Almost Becomes a Detective

*T*here were three things that Granddaddy Davis loved to read: the Holy Bible, the *Congressional Record,* and the *Atlanta Constitution.*

Joel Chandler Harris was editor of the *Atlanta Constitution,* and when the Sunday issue finally arrived (at least a week later) by mail in Iron Duff, the paper was read and reread until, now much softer than the Sears and Roebuck catalog pages, it was delegated to final service in the outhouse.

When Uncle Frank was a thirteen-year-old, he didn't care much about hearing either the news or the editorials in the *Constitution,* but he did dearly love to look at the advertisements in that big, wonderful newspaper.

In addition to modern equipment, clothing, and appliances, he especially loved the ads for everything from miracle cures to self-help courses which seemed to cluster on the back pages of the Sunday paper.

Uncle Frank saw advertisements that promised to cure baldness and impotence with the same elixir. He read about a correspondence course that would teach you to be a famous artist. He saw ads for remedies to cure gout and dropsy and warts and dandruff. He saw an advertised home-study course which would enable you to learn locksmithing.

All these advertisements were interesting. They were symbolic of a magical and unreal world far beyond the bounds of Iron Duff.

One day, however, Uncle Frank spotted an ad on the back page of the *Constitution* that captured him on the spot. It was an offer for a home-study *detective* course, complete in six lessons. The course kit contained a fake beard disguise, a magnifying glass, and an undercover detective badge "for only nineteen dollars and ninety-five cents—including a certificate suitable for framing!"

With great excitement, he approached Granddaddy.

"You've always told us that we could be anything in the world we wanted to be if we would just try hard enough. I have just found what I want to be more than anything else in the world."

"What is it, son?" Granddaddy asked.

"A detective," Uncle Frank answered, and held up the nineteen-dollar-and-ninety-five-cent newspaper advertisement.

"I want to be a detective a *lot* more than Abraham Lincoln wanted to be a lawyer. I'll work to pay you back the money, too."

That proposal didn't get very far. Granddaddy didn't object to Uncle Frank's ordering the home-study course or to his plans for life as a detective, but the education for his new career would have to be paid for in advance. No loans to be paid back later.

And so, propelled by the exciting prospect of becoming the Sherlock Holmes of Iron Duff, Uncle Frank set to work to come up with jobs which might provide him with funds for his education.

This was difficult. In the first place, no one in Iron Duff seemed to need any unskilled thirteen-year-old labor. Then, there was just no market for the extra eggs (everybody seemed to have their own chickens), and it was the wrong season of the year for digging ginseng.

The only way Uncle Frank could come up with to raise cash was to trap rabbits and sell their skins to the hide man in Clyde. At the going rate, it would take seventy-eight rabbit skins to yield the nineteen dollars and ninety-five cents—if he saved every single cent.

Undaunted, Uncle Frank assembled four rabbit gums from scrap wood, set them out at four different but likely looking places he could easily check each day, baited them with leftovers, and waited.

Progress was slow. He caught two rabbits the first week. It was work to skin them and stretch the hides on boards to dry, and clean the rest for Grandmother to cook. Only seventy-six more rabbits to go!

In spite of the story Uncle Frank in later years told the Crown Feed boys, he *did* go to school during these days, along with his brothers and sisters. The four rabbit traps were placed along the route taken to and from school so that they could more easily be checked in coming and going each day.

School was an interesting proposition in and of itself. The teacher was Uncle Grover, the older half-brother to Uncle Frank and the younger batch of Davis brothers and sisters. The schoolhouse was a one-room affair, and Granddaddy tried to help the children overcome the intimate problems associated with having their own older brother for the teacher by insisting that they all address him as *Mister* Grover. Uncle Grover did his part in the same wise by wearing a white shirt, a hand-tied bow tie, and a double-breasted black suit to school each day. This offered him more separation from his pupils.

Overall, the arrangement seemed to work quite well.

As the rabbit-trapping continued, winter came on, and though it was sunny in the afternoon on most days, the morning walks to school grew colder and colder.

In addition to being the teacher, Uncle Grover's responsibilities at school included his being the janitor and all-around maintenance man. It fell on him to cut the wood and build the fire in the big, pot-bellied stove to warm up the schoolhouse each morning. Once all the children were there, and as the day warmed up, the fire was allowed to burn out.

Uncle Grover usually laid the fire for the next morning before leaving school in the afternoon. This was beneficial in two ways. First, it meant the fire was all ready to light as soon as he got to school in the morning, and second, if he was going to get his professor's uniform dirty, he did so in the afternoon before going home instead of in the morning when he would look less than neat all through the day.

It was a sunny day in early December when all the children left school, and Uncle Grover laid the fire in the stove in preparation for the next day.

He had appropriated a little stack of old *Atlanta Constitutions* (after all, you only need so many sheets of paper in the outhouse) as part of his stack of kindling.

He shook the stove grate until all the cold ashes fell down into the cinderbox, then began with a loosely wadded pile of newspaper. On top went a tent of small kindling and finally some heavier sticks. Now he was ready for the morning.

Uncle Grover latched the door behind him (there was no lock) and headed for home.

While all this was happening, Uncle Frank, assisted by his older brother Harry, was busy checking the rabbit traps. The first two were empty and the bait undisturbed, but the door of the third was shut. They could hear something inside struggling to get out.

"You've got a big one, it sounds like," Uncle Harry commented. Then both of them heard an angry *"Mee-ooow-ww!"* come from inside the wooden box.

"Aw," Uncle Frank lamented, "it's not a rabbit. It's an old tomcat."

It was indeed a big, black tomcat. They could see it reach a paw out through a crack on the side of the rabbit-trap, like it could find some way to open the box from the outside. The cat was making so much noise and scratching around so madly that Uncle Frank and Uncle Harry decided it must have been trapped in there most of the day.

They started to open the box and let the cat out, but they didn't.

Neither one knew exactly where the idea came from. Neither one would ever admit, even to the other, that they came up with this thought on their own. It was one of those ideas which just seem to drop out of the sky and hit you with such force that you have to listen to them.

"Don't just let a good tomcat loose!" the idea seemed to say. "Now that you've got it, figure out something worthwhile to do with it!"

Uncle Harry was the first one to voice the thought. "Frank, we shouldn't just let a good tomcat go to waste. We ought to find some good way to use it."

So, as the tomcat grew wilder, the two of them discussed the animal's destiny.

No one knows whether they could see the road from where they were and, perhaps, on seeing Uncle Grover pass by on the way home realized that the schoolhouse was empty. Or maybe it was another message from heaven. At any rate, they decided that this was one tomcat who needed to spend some time in school.

It took both Uncle Frank and Uncle Harry to comfortably carry the long, square rabbit trap full of tomcat back to the schoolhouse. Uncle Harry pushed open the schoolhouse door, and they went inside with their load. The door was pushed shut and Uncle Harry started to release the cat.

Again there was a pause. "Wait a minute, Harry," Uncle Frank said. "As upset as that tomcat is, he'll scratch our eyes out if we let him loose right in here with us. And after that, he's liable to escape when we try to get back out the door. How are we going to let him out?"

The two boys thought about it for a minute, and Uncle Frank himself solved the problem. "Look," he said to his brother, Harry, and pointed to the big pot-bellied stove. "The door on the front of that stove is not much bigger than the end of this rabbit box. I know what we can do.

"Let's lift up the stove door. Then we'll hold the trap up against the stove. We can just ease the trip-door up, and the tomcat can jump right into the stove and we can drop the stove door *fast!*

"He can spend the night in the stove, and Mister Grover will let him out when he comes to light the fire in the morning!"

And so it was done.

The tomcat seemed to glad to leave the rabbit box for the larger space the stove offered, but having thought he was on his way to freedom, he sounded even wilder and more upset than ever when the stove door clanked shut and he found himself in a world of firewood, ashes, and soot.

Followed by the sounds of jumping, meowing, and spitting, Uncle Frank and Uncle Harry quickly left the school. They reset the rabbit trap where it had been before and struck out for home.

At the supper table, the entire family was present: all the younger children, Granddaddy and Grandmother, and their teacher-brother, Mister Grover. It was a good, long supper of both eating and talking. Finally the conversation worked its way around to the rabbit-trapping business.

"Frank," Granddaddy asked, "how are you progressing with your detective-course money? I've seen a few rabbit skins stretched out in the barn. How many do you have to go?"

"I'm making progress," the optimistic boy answered. "I've just got to catch and skin seventy-one more rabbits and I'll be done. I've already caught *seven!*"

"Well, son," Granddaddy smiled, "at that rate you'll be grown up before you get to be a detective. That rabbit catching's a slow way to make money."

"I have to do it, Granddaddy." Uncle Frank stuck his thirteen-year-old lip out. "You won't loan it to me."

"I've been thinking about that," Granddaddy said. "You've really been sticking with this detective idea. I don't want to waste my money, but if you could come up with the solution to a few crimes right here in Iron Duff on your own, I might decide that putting twenty dollars into that detective course for you could be a good investment. Start keeping your eyes open for crime, son."

Uncle Frank was encouraged and disheartened at the same time. Granddaddy had opened the door a crack, but there just was not a lot of crime to be solved in Iron Duff.

Still, that night, Uncle Frank fell asleep with renewed dreams of becoming a detective.

The next morning, Uncle Grover was up and dressed in his professor uniform, fresh, white shirt included, before any of the other children ever got up. When they got to the kitchen, he was on his way out the door to school.

He left early for two reasons: the spoken one was to prepare the room and light the fire before any of the pupils arrived. The unspoken one was to be sure none of the other children saw him walking to school with his own brothers and sisters.

It was a cold and frosty December morning. The clarity of the sunrise gave promise that the day would warm up later, but Uncle Grover knew he would need to light the fire in the stove at school. As it was a good two-mile walk to get there, he stuck his hands in his pockets and walked faster.

Once at school, Uncle Grover got ready. He took off his suit coat so that if he did get any soot on him, it would be on the washable white shirt and not on coat. He pulled two sheets of newspaper off the topmost copy of the stack of old newspapers which he had brought to school for this very purpose and rolled the papers into a loose cone.

He pulled a wooden match from his pocket, struck it on the side of the pot-bellied stove, held it to the edge of the newspaper cone until it ignited, and then he slowly turned the paper until it was burning well.

Inside the stove, the exhausted tomcat had fallen asleep until the scratch of the wooden match against the stove awakened him with the knowledge that *something* was about to happen. By now, the cat was ready for anything.

Uncle Grover stepped up to the stove, and with one smooth and practiced motion, lifted the stove door and pushed the burning newspaper inside to light the fire he had carefully laid the afternoon before.

The tomcat was all ready and set to go, and when the burning newspaper came into the stove with him, he shot off his mark. Covered with all the soot of a full night of stove residence, the big cat leaped straight out of the stove and straight onto Uncle Grover's fresh white shirt.

Before Uncle Grover knew what had hit him, the cat went straight through the nearest window leaving nothing but a trail of soot, broken glass, and cat hair behind.

While all this had been happening, the younger children were on their way to school, with no one but Harry and Frank knowing that anything might be going on there other than preparation for a normal day of school.

Suddenly they began to hear the sound of a bell—a sound which was steadily moving closer and closer to them.

As they rounded a curve in the road, they met Mister Grover. He walked fast, looking at the ground, with his suit coat drawn tightly around him. In his right hand was the hand-held school bell.

As he passed them and continued on toward home, he rang the bell over and over again as he spoke to whoever would listen: "School's out...school's out...school's out..."

It was a full week before notice was sent around that school was reopening again.

At the supper table several days later, the subject of Uncle Frank's detective-course money-raising came up again. Granddaddy asked, "How's the rabbit trapping coming, Frank?"

"Not so bad, not so bad," the boy reported. "I caught four during that week that school was out. I only have sixty-seven more to go to meet my goal. If I could find some crime around here to solve, I could order it a whole lot sooner."

"I've been thinking about that too, Frank," Granddaddy said, "and I've got another offer to make to you."

"What's that?" Uncle Frank was curious.

"If you could figure out who put that tomcat in the stove at school, why I'd be willing to order that detective course for you right off, and you wouldn't even have to pay me back. How about that?"

At that very moment, Uncle Frank's vocational plans changed.

Later on he told us that was the very day when he decided to be a farmer, right there on the spot!

# Little Buchanan Outruns the Law

*B*ack during the Second World War, hitchhiking was an accepted way of youthful travel. With so many military bases in the Carolinas and coastal Virginia, there were always young, uniformed servicemen on leave to be seen by the highway with their thumbs stuck out. They often carried small cardboard signs with destinations such as "Nashville" or "Kentucky" grease-pencilled on them in hopes of catching an extended ride.

Such hitchhikers were gladly offered rides by drivers who had members of their own families away from home due to the war.

As the 1950s unrolled, however, hitchhiking lost some of its acceptability. There seemed to be an increasing number of news stories about what I heard the grown-ups call "incidents" involving hitchhikers.

My father and Uncle Frank began to advise all of us against thumbing a ride anywhere, because even though we knew most of the cars and drivers in Haywood County, you never could tell when a big-city stranger, up to no good, might come through just trying to pick up a load of trouble.

None of the adults I knew ever picked up hitchhikers unless it was someone we knew. Even when they did stop to offer someone a ride, the person picked up was usually just walking somewhere rather than thumbing to begin with. We picked them up because we knew them.

One day in the fall of the year, Uncle Frank needed to go over to Sylva to see about buying some equipment from a dairyman who was selling out his business. Since it was a Saturday and I didn't have anything in particular to do, he invited me to ride along with him and I went.

He came by our house, stopped in for a cup of coffee, and with it being by now late in the morning, we started on our way to Sylva in his yellow 1949 Mercury.

The road to Sylva ran out through Hazelwood, past Dayton Rubber Company, up through Saunook, and finally over Balsam Gap before dropping down into Jackson County.

We drove along without seeing anything interesting to talk about until we were about halfway up through Saunook toward Balsam Gap. Then, just as the yellow Mercury rounded a curve, we saw a teenage boy standing beside the road just ahead of us.

He was well dressed in a red blazer and necktie, with his right thumb extended in search of a ride and his left hand firmly holding a big suitcase crossed by a red and white N.C. State sticker.

I expected to feel the yellow Mercury speed up and to hear a few derogatory remarks about the dangers of hitchhiking as we sped past. It was a great surprise when I felt the big car begin to slow down and realized that Uncle Frank was going to offer the boy a ride.

"I thought you didn't believe in hitchhiking," I said to him.

He looked back at me and smiled. "I don't," he answered. "It's dangerous. And this young man's not going to believe in it anymore either once this ride is over." I knew I was getting ready to observe education in action.

By this time, the car had eased to a stop beside the fresh State student. Uncle Frank leaned across me and rolled down the window.

"Do you need a ride, son? How far are you going?"

"I sure do. I'm on my way home over between Sylva and Dillsboro. I've been on the road all night, since yesterday afternoon."

"Climb in the back," Uncle Frank instructed him. "Stick your suitcase right on in there with you. We're going your way, and you might as well go along with us."

The back door of the yellow Mercury opened. The N.C. State suitcase entered first, followed by the red-coated hitchhiker. Then the door slammed shut.

Uncle Frank was usually a very calm driver. Suddenly, however, he pulled the Mercury's gear shift into low, hit the gas and popped the clutch. Two showers of gravel left the rear wheels, both of which squealed loudly as they reached the edge of the pavement. The new rider was glued back against the rear seat as the yellow car swerved, then straightened out, then accelerated toward Balsam Gap.

It seemed to me like we were driving awfully fast, and on top of that, Uncle Frank was just using one hand. With his free hand, he flipped out a pack of cigarette papers, licked one loose from the packet, and proceeded to roll a cigarette with one hand (and his mouth) as he drove full speed with the other. At the same time, he looked back and engaged the new rider in conversation.

"I saw your suitcase," he said. "Do you go to State College?"

I sure do," the boy said, seeming to hope that answering all of this man's questions might at least get him to watch the road while driving. "I'm a freshman. This is my first trip home since I went down to Raleigh in August. The folks don't know I'm coming home—it's a surprise!"

"A surprise, huh? So what you mean to say is that they don't know where you are right now? They wouldn't even know to start looking for you if something bad happened?"

"Well, I *am* almost home!" the boy answered. He seemed to be getting a little bit nervous. He looked at me like I was some sort of safety guarantee. I stared back at him as if I didn't even understand the conversation.

"What's your name, son?" Uncle Frank asked gruffly.

"Buchanan," the boy answered. "Everybody calls me 'Junior' so they can keep me and Daddy apart."

With that information, Uncle Frank knew exactly who we were hauling. Jackson County was full of Buchanans, and the one in our back seat was the very grandson of the man we were going to buy dairy equipment from.

"Well, Junior," Uncle Frank went on , "how do you like it down in Raleigh?"

We were nearly to Balsam Gap now, and I was not looking forward to our descent of the other side of the mountain with Uncle Frank driving like this.

"Oh, it's OK." Little Buchanan was fairly sweating now and holding on to the armrest for dear life as he tried to anticipate the direction in which the yellow car would swerve next. "It's a pretty big city. I don't get very far off of campus, though, so I don't know much about it."

"Well," Uncle Frank continued, "I used to live in Raleigh myself."

This was news to me. I knew Uncle Frank had been in Wilmington at the shipyard during the war, but I had never heard at all of his ever living in Raleigh. I listened with interest as he went on.

"Yes sir, I lived down there *three* different times. I never did care much for it though."

"What did you do there?" Little Buchanan asked, trying to pretend he was in a normal environment.

"I was in manufacturing for a while, and another time I was in food service, and finally I was in the laundry business. None of them ever did amount to much, though."

Now I knew something funny was going on. I had never heard any of this at all.

"Well," the boy went on, "where did you live down there? I mean, I don't know much about Raleigh, but if it was close to the State campus, I might even know where you lived."

"Aw, son," Uncle Frank answered him, "it was in a part of town you wouldn't know anything about."

"I might." Little Buchanan puffed up. "I have been around some, you know."

"Well, son," Uncle Frank said while he rolled another cigarette and drove at the same time, "I don't just volunteer to tell most people this, but since you asked, my places of residence and my places of employment *were* close to the State campus, in fact, right out there on Western Boulevard. Junior, you asked, and so I'll tell you. I've served three terms down at Raleigh at State Prison. Yes sir, the first time I made license plates, the second time I worked in the kitchen, and the third time they stuck me in the laundry."

Little Buchanan was pale as a sheet and seemed to be shaking a little, though the way the car was weaving, it was hard to tell for sure.

"State Prison? What were you in there for?"

By now I had to look at my feet and nearly hold my breath to keep from laughing out loud. I made a good effort, though, because I wanted to hear the answer to this question.

"The first time I was down there because I borrowed a car from a feller and then just plumb forgot to take it back. Why, shoot, boy, once I sold it I couldn't have taken it back anyway, now could I?"

"No, sir!" Little Buchanan was afraid to hear any more of the answer to his question, but it was coming anyway.

"The second time, they asked me to go down there was after I borrowed this woman to cook and clean house for me. Her daddy and her husband both got right nasty about that, and she couldn't even cook, but the judge sent me to Raleigh anyhow. Funny thing was that this time, they didn't let me make no more license plates but put *me* to cooking. That was good punishment for a lot of people!"

"Lord God!" Little Buchanan was dripping sweat. "What in the world did you do the third time?"

Uncle Frank turned around and stared straight at Little Buchanan while the yellow Mercury zoomed down the road. He grinned broadly, with the home-rolled cigarette hanging out of the corner of his mouth.

"I cut a feller's head off with a butcher knife. It was all right, though. He was dead. I killed him first—he was a friend of mine!"

If Little Buchanan hadn't been so scared, he would have fainted right on the spot. Something inside told him that he better stay conscious no matter what, with this crazy man around.

"You *killed* a *friend* of yours?" Little Buchanan did everything but roll over with his feet in the air as he wiped the sweat from his forehead with the sleeve of his red blazer.

"Well, son, you don't think I would kill somebody I don't even *know*, do you? I know better than that; I go to Sunday School! Yes sir, that last time the judge sent me to live in Raleigh, they wouldn't even let me *cook* anymore. They made me work in the laundry."

Finally Little Buchanan recovered his senses just enough to ask his next question. "Mister," he began cautiously, "if you killed a man and cut his head off, how come you're back out of prison now?"

Uncle Frank looked straight at him and grinned his widest grin. "Son," he almost whispered to him, "that's exactly what *they'd* like to know down there in Raleigh. Why, son, I broke out of there, and I'll never tell how or go back alive. They're looking for me now, but I've got a double-barrelled sawed-off twelve-gauge shotgun under this front seat that will insure that I either stay out of there or die trying. You help me keep on the lookout, will you? I reckon they're looking for me all over North Carolina!"

About that time, the yellow Mercury rounded a curve and entered the last straight stretch of road before Sylva.

There was a little drive-in restaurant by the side of the road in the middle of that straight stretch, and Uncle Frank knew that the Sheriff, the Sylva Police, and the local Highway Patrol were in the habit of meeting there for coffee about mid-morning on Saturday. He peered ahead, and sure enough, he saw five law enforcement vehicles parked beside the roadway up ahead. They were all backed in so they could leave in a hurry if anyone got an emergency call.

He slammed on the brakes and slid the Mercury sideways in the road, throwing Little Buchanan into the floorboard. As the boy, shaking for sure now, pulled himself up until he could see over the seat, Uncle Frank started hollering at him.

"Oh-my-gosh, Junior, there's all the law in Jackson County! I knew they were looking for me, but I didn't expect the showdown to come this soon. Son, get out of here and run for it... I'll try to cover you 'til you get to the woods— this is not your fight! Now get out of here and *run like you've never run before!*"

The back door of the Mercury popped open and Junior Buchanan and his N.C. State suitcase disappeared, leaving the door standing open behind them.

Uncle Frank had stopped the Mercury exactly at the bottom of a big grade cut for the highway, and the escape route to the woods was a steep clay bank more than fifty feet high.

As Junior climbed the bank, dragging the suitcase, red clay flying everywhere, Uncle Frank leaned toward the open car door and hollered, "Run…run…run!"

As soon as the boy was out of sight in the woods, we went on to the drive-in restaurant. Uncle Frank and I walked inside to where the sheriff was. Uncle Frank knew him well.

"Sheriff Tate," he said, "young Junior Buchanan's back up there in the woods at the top of that last road-grade cut. He's trying to get home to surprise his mama and daddy. I expect he'll need a ride in a little while, and I don't believe he'll be thumbing for it. Reckon you could get him on home? He might be talking kind of crazy—he's been coming from Raleigh ever since yesterday, so just take him on to his mama and don't pay much attention to anything he says."

The sheriff knew Uncle Frank well, too. With no questions asked, he smiled and nodded his head.

# Uncle Frank and the Snake Guineas

*T*he *Waynesville Mountaineer* was published twice a week when I was growing up in Haywood County. It was the premier newspaper in the western end of the county while the *Canton Enterprise* served the eastern end. The only daily news had to come through the *Asheville Citizen,* and that was hardly considered local.

The *Mountaineer* regularly hired young reporters, many of them fresh out of journalism school at Chapel Hill. Most of these fledgling writers served a short term at the biweekly paper before moving on to a larger city.

Uncle Frank was always interested in helping young people get started in their life's work, including those young members of the press whose names from time to time appeared attached to articles in the *Mountaineer.* He often helped guide them toward newsworthy events and in the direction of interesting features.

One day, he had stopped at our house on his way to do an errand and was looking at the *Mountaineer* when he started laughing.

"Look, Joe," he said to my daddy. "They've got a new reporter at the newspaper, and as usual, they're publishing everything he writes. Well, that's one way to teach them."

"What's this one done that's so funny?" Daddy asked.

"Look at this article," he laughed. "Titled 'How to Milk a Cow.' Listen to this: 'The cow's milk is made accessible through four protuberances called "teats" which project forth from the lower portion of her udder. One begins by grasping the two nearer teats with one's clean hands.'"

We were all laughing by now. Why, here was some boy from the city thinking that he could tell Haywood County farm boys and girls the most basic thing all of them knew: how to milk!

"Frank," Daddy continued, "I believe this one really does need some educating. Do you have any ideas on the subject?"

"Not now," he replied, "but I surely will think about it. And you're right...this one needs it bad!"

Uncle Frank was on his way over to Henderson County to see a man about buying a dozen guinea eggs.

Back when he and my daddy had been little boys, everybody in Iron Duff and most of Haywood County had a small flock of guinea hens. The hens ran loose and fended for themselves, and in addition to laying little eggs with shells much harder than hen eggs, the guinea hens were wonderful watchdogs.

They would roost in a tree above the road near the house. They very quickly came to know exactly who belonged in the household to which they were attached. If anyone else, friend or foe, happened to approach the house at night, the guinea hens would make a racket that would put the finest guard dog to shame. No one in any rural area felt as safe as they did when they had a flock of watch guineas on duty.

It had been years now since anyone in Iron Duff or the surrounding communities had had any guinea hens. But as Uncle Frank was politicking more and more and leaving Aunt Kathleen at home alone many evenings, it occurred to him that he would just feel a lot better about her being there by herself if they had a flock of watch guineas.

He searched the want ads in the *Asheville Citizen* to no avail and finally came upon an advertisement in the *State* magazine notifying anyone interested that a certain farmer outside Hendersonville had guineas and would sell eggs for hatching.

Uncle Frank had waited until one of his Plymouth Rocks went to setting on the creekbank, and with a hen to do his hatching work, he called the man in Henderson County and was, on this very day, on the way to get a dozen eggs to start his new brood of watch guineas.

With one more laugh over "How to Milk a Cow," we told him goodbye and secured a promise that he would let us know all about how the guineas did and what kind of ideas he came up with to help educate the new newspaper reporter.

It was late in the afternoon when Uncle Frank got home to Iron Duff. The eggs had been wrapped in a couple of heavy towels to keep them warm on the ride home. Now Uncle Frank got my cousin Frances to help him chase the old setting hen off of her creekside nest and keep her away while he carefully substituted the twelve guinea eggs for the eggs of her own that she was hatching. It was plumb dark by the time the job was done and the eggs were safe in the care of a hatching expert.

Every day or two, Daddy called Uncle Frank to find out whether the eggs had hatched or not. As neither of them could remember whether guinea eggs hatched in the same time as chicken eggs, they had to keep a close lookout.

About ten days after the eggs had been placed under the Plymouth Rock, we had a startling report from Uncle Frank.

Whenever he went out to check on the eggs, he went when the old hen was off and he could examine the nest without danger of being attacked. This afternoon, she was gone, but when he looked in the nest, something terrible was in her place.

A big blacksnake had crawled into the nest and swallowed every single one of those guinea eggs. The snake was still curled up in the nest, and Uncle Frank could see the eggs, not a single one of them broken, lined up like twelve bumps on a log, running a good part of the length of that snake. He was filled with terrible dismay.

Then, he told us, seeing that the swallowed eggs were not broken, he had an idea.

Taking out his pocket knife, he grabbed the full and now sluggish black snake. He turned it over on its back, slit it open all along its belly, removed the twelve apparently unharmed guinea eggs, and replaced them in the hen's nest. The dead snake got tossed down the creekbank.

He hid across the creek and watched for the hen's return. She would have no idea in the world of the trauma her future stepchildren had endured. She came back and set.

Everyone waited anxiously to find out whether the eggs, swallowed by and retrieved from a blacksnake, would actually hatch.

Uncle Frank called the following Saturday to report that the guineas had, indeed, hatched—every single one of them.

"But," he said, "I've got a whole lot more to tell you than that. Do you know what?" he asked.

"What?" Daddy asked for all of us.

"You might not believe it over the telephone, Joe, but every last one of these baby guineas has got a forked tongue—just exactly like that snake that swallowed them.

"And that's not all. You can even tell the order in which they were swallowed. The first one swallowed is pure white—scared the color right out of him. The next one is just a little bit speckled and the next and the next a little more so. Why, the last one was so eager to be in there with his brothers and sisters that he has his full, natural color. He wasn't scared at all!"

Daddy was laughing so hard that he could hardly pass on to us what Uncle Frank way saying; he almost dropped the telephone.

Finally he said, "That's good, Frank. In fact, that's so good, I think you ought to try to get it written up in the paper so everybody in the county can hear about it."

This thought came from Daddy as a joke, but it hit Uncle Frank as the perfect story for that new "How to Milk a Cow" reporter to get his hands on. They talked about that idea for a few minutes, and then Uncle Frank began to work on his plan.

Early Monday morning, he called the editor of the *Mountaineer,* an old friend of his, and told him he had a story for the paper's new reporter, Mr. Sharpe. The editor put the young man right on the line after guaranteeing Uncle Frank full editorial cooperation.

"Hello, son," Uncle Frank began. "I've been reading your articles in the paper, and I find them very interesting. Why, that feature about milking just warmed my heart!"

The young reporter seemed, even over the telephone, to glow with pride.

"Now, Mr. Sharpe, we've had a very strange occurrence here on my farm. I called the editor himself about it this morning, thinking he probably handles all the big stories himself, but he suggested that I talk with you. Says you're good at stuff like this. Are you interested?"

"Well, Mr. Davis, as a reporter, I'm interested in everything. What did you say this story is about? Something strange happened there? Can you tell me more about it?"

"You wouldn't believe it, Mr. Sharpe," Uncle Frank went on. "I think you just better get on out here as fast as you can, and be sure to bring a camera. We've got the potential for some Pulitzer Prize winning photographs here. Hurry, now, Mr. Sharpe."

"I'm on the way. Where do you live, Mr. Davis? Just tell me how to get there!"

Uncle Frank spent the next ten minutes giving Mr. Sharpe a set of circuitous directions which would take him on most of the roads in Haywood County before he finally arrived in Iron Duff. Then he said, "You've only got about an hour at the most, so get on it!"

As Mr. Sharpe flew out the door of the newspaper office, the editor called to him, "You pay good attention to Mr. Davis. He knows what he's talking about!"

It was nearly two and one-half hours and nobody knows how many miles later when Mr. Sharpe finally came driving down the road to the farm at Iron Duff. Uncle Frank was waiting out in the yard, nearly jumping up and down with excitement (or so it appeared to Mr. Sharpe).

"Where have you been, son?" he asked, seeming very upset, when Mr. Sharpe got out of the car.

"I've been coming as fast as I could, why I never even stopped, Mr. Davis. I didn't know Haywood County was this big! But I'm here now. What in the world is this big story all about?"

The entire saga of the guineas was described by Uncle Frank in exquisite detail, beginning with a history of guinea hens and ending with the remarkable incidence of forked tongues and progressive albinism. Mr. Sharpe took notes so fast his pencil lead got hot. This was the most interesting thing he had ever heard in all his brief career.

At last Uncle Frank was done. Mr. Sharpe caught up with his notes and sat back for a moment, just letting the magnificence of what he had just written soak in.

Then he got excited again. "Where are they, Mr. Davis? I brought the camera, just like you said. It's the big one from the newspaper office. I've got to get pictures of these things!"

"Well, son,"—Uncle Frank looked at him seriously— "you know I told you to get here just as fast as you could, didn't I?"

"You did, Mr. Davis, and I came as fast as I could. But it was such a long way."

"Well, that's too bad. That's why I was so upset when you finally got here. Mr. Sharpe, you are just thirty minutes too late."

"Too late?" the young man fairly lamented. "What am I too late for? What happened?"

"Son," Uncle Frank said sympathetically, "it was the poultry engineers."

"Poultry engineers? What poultry engineers?"

"Let me tell you." Uncle Frank tried to sound calm. "I had a team of poultry engineers come in here early this morning from North Carolina State College. I had been waiting for them for several weeks now to adjust the settings on my mechanical roosters. They had them aimed a little bit too high.

"Well, son, the truth is that when the poultry engineers saw those snake guineas, they just *had* to take them back to Raleigh to study them. One of them told me secretly they might be able to get them on display at the World's Fair. Now wouldn't that be something?

"So, Mr. Sharpe, I've told you the entire story, but you're just a little too late to get the pictures to go with it. Better luck next time."

With that Mr. Sharpe headed back to town. After all, it was a long drive, and he had a deadline to meet in order to get this wonderful story into the first-of-the-week edition of the biweekly.

The editor of the *Mountaineer* was true to his word. The next day, readers all over Haywood County (the west end at least) saw a headline which read, "Davis's Forked-Tongue Guineas to Appear at World's Fair."

The next week, however, the same people read that Mr. Sharpe had left the *Mountaineer*. It seems he had found a new job writing for a tabloid in New York City.

# Uncle Frank and the Talking Cat

*M*any years ago, a Scotsman by the name of Marshall MacReadie came to live in Iron Duff.

He begged a tiny square of land high on the Kansada Mountain, built himself a small log cabin, and proceeded to eke out a living by offering his labor for the jobs no one else wanted to do.

He could be counted on to help with the terrible-smelling job of leather tanning. He was the one to wash the chitterlings when hogs were killed. He would rebuild outhouses and dispose of dead animals, and though his pay for these tasks was small, he seemed to save every cent he made.

Marshall MacReadie knew exactly when to drop in for a meal and precisely when to glean harvested fields for produce he had never worked to grow.

Everyone in Iron Duff knew MacReadie, and one or another often asked him what he was saving his money for. He had a ready answer.

"When I've enuff," he said in his growly burr, "I'll be sendin' back to th' auld countree for a proper wife...my family in Ayrshire will find one for me!"

He worked and saved for six or seven years before sending to the old country. After more than six months of waiting, Anna arrived.

She was a pale and hollow-eyed girl who could not have been more than sixteen years old. She seemed to be starved, so that she would grab at food like an animal, and her speech was so broguish that no one but Marshall himself could half understand her.

People wondered, could this be the wife sent to Mac-Readie by his family after so long? Had they taken his money and sent him some orphan child who knew no better? Had there been some great mistake?

Though she seemed frail and wan, Anna proved to be equal to life with Marshall MacReadie. Whenever they were seen on the road, she was always the one walking in front, and when people inquired about hiring MacReadie, he often answered, "I'll have to talk with Anna first."

It was neither politeness nor consideration which produced such behavior, it seems, but pure fear on MacReadie's part. He began now and then to tell strange tales of her habits and powers and did not disagree when some of those few neighbors who seemed to know them both well suggested that Anna might be a witch.

Soon the general opinion was that Anna, now no longer frail but having the appearance of strong leather, did indeed have powers which no one in Iron Duff wanted to deal with.

The only thing she seemed to have no power over at all was Marshall MacReadie's money.

He still worked and he still saved. Anna could not wrest from him more than the most meager allowance for the necessities of living. She was often seen scratching after other families' leftover turnips or grubbing for missed Irish potatoes.

After almost twenty years more of saving, Marshall MacReadie made the second major expenditure of his life.

He took nearly all of his savings and placed an order for his own tombstone!

Everybody in Iron Duff heard about it before they saw it. He ordered it from a monument maker in Asheville, and when it was ready, he borrowed my granddaddy's wagon and team to go to bring it home.

Since he asked for no help, no one knew how he managed to unload it. The first time any of his neighbors saw it, the new marker was standing on the front porch of old Marshall's little log cabin.

It was a tall granite marker with the a simple inscription "Marshall MacReadie" on the one side and "Rest in Peace" on the other. No one knew which side was the front.

Old Marshall was right proud for people to come by and look at the tombstone. He kept it oiled and shined up and kept the weeds cut down from around the porch so it was easy to see. He told people it seemed a shame to wait until you're dead to get your tombstone and then not ever get to enjoy it the way other people do after you're gone.

That made fair sense to everyone except Anna. All she could see in the tombstone was twenty years of short groceries! She felt as if she had purchased the tombstone with her own poverty and starvation, and she hated the pure sight of the thing. She could not abide hearing it admired either by Marshall or any of his visiting neighbors.

"'Rest In Peace,' my bad eye," she was once heard to say. "There'll be no peace for Mister MacReadie above or below that tombstone as long as I have anything to do with it."

Since she did have something to do with it, there was no peace for Marshall from the day the big stone was installed on the front porch.

Uncle Frank and Uncle Harry, both half-grown boys at the time, were awfully curious about old Marshall's tombstone, but partly because he did not want to raise

Anna's ire, Granddaddy would not let the boys go up on the mountain to have a look at it. A year or two passed, and the initial excitement about the tombstone had about worn down in Iron Duff, but the curiosity of these two boys was undiminished. They had had no chance at all to see what they had heard everyone talk about.

One day in the spring of the year, Uncle Frank couldn't take it any longer. About fifteen years old now, his curiosity seemed to rise in the spring right along with the sap of the trees. He decided it was time for him to go up on the Kansada and see that tombstone.

He wouldn't even tell his brother Harry. It was so scary to do something Granddaddy had stoutly prohibited that he was afraid even to tell Harry. He would slip up on the mountain on his own.

He picked a day when Granddaddy had gone to town, and after breakfast, he volunteered to wash the dishes without even being asked. He figured that if he got in Grandmother's way for a while, she would be relieved to have him out of sight the rest of the morning.

When the dishes were done and he saw that she was busy with her churning, he wandered past the barn and then lit off toward the Kansada.

The day had been fairly clear when he left the house, but as he walked, a cloud-front came over the Kansada and turned the world dark and gray and chilly. Still, he walked on.

About halfway up through Jolly Cove, Uncle Frank heard a rustling in the laurel bushes along beside the road. He stopped in his tracks and peered into the thick bushes. He saw there the biggest black cat he had ever seen. Its eyes glowed green, and it stared straight back at him without blinking.

Finally, knowing that an old cat couldn't hurt anybody, he turned from its stare and continued his walk up the Kansada.

Very soon, a sound behind let him know the black cat was following. The light was now very dim in the woods, but it was too late to turn back. Without ever looking at the cat, he continued on up to where he knew Marshall Mac-Readie lived.

As soon as he came into the clearing where the cabin was, he knew that something was wrong. The tombstone was not on the cabin porch, and he could see something lying in the weeds beside the porch.

As he drew closer to the house, he saw that there in the weeds at the edge of the porch lay Marshall MacReadie, stone, cold dead. He had been crushed to death by the huge, granite tombstone which covered almost all of his body except his head and feet. Uncle Frank could see that the edge of the porch had collapsed. MacReadie must have been admiring the big granite marker at the very moment it had fallen on him.

Uncle Frank turned to run for help, though he knew that old Marshall was far beyond help that any living soul could offer him.

When he turned, he saw that the cabin clearing was ringed by black cats. He shivered, and felt his body fill with panic. The cats made no move toward the house. In a moment, they silently melted into the woods and disappeared.

Because of the great excitement at the news he brought, Uncle Frank was not punished for going up on the Kansada Mountain to Marshall's house after Granddaddy had told him not to. His brother Harry was fascinated by the story he told. Yet, partly because he had not been there, there were several points in Uncle Frank's telling which Harry tried to act as though he doubted.

It took a team of mules and a block-and-tackle tied to a big oak tree to tilt the tombstone off old Marshall's dead body. Speculation was that the cabin porch was simply not strong enough to hold the tombstone and that it was merely a matter of coincidence that MacReadie had been standing there when it had fallen.

It was a strange thing, though, that Anna was nowhere to be found. Uncle Frank had not even noticed that he hadn't seen her at the cabin when he found old Marshall. With all those black cats around, he was not paying attention to who *wasn't* there. He was too busy getting away from who—or what—was.

Anna was not to be found in all of Iron Duff. No one had seen her for days, and her absence was a mystery. As mysterious as it was, her disappearance did not disappoint some people. With her vow to see that old Marshall *never* rested in peace, people thought it would probably be easier to give him a quiet and proper burial with her not present.

And so, plans were made for his burial. A coffin was built, the big tombstone was hauled to the cemetery, and after a foodless wake and an emotionless service, he was buried at the very top of the graveyard.

No one seemed to think they should bother about adding the date of Marshall's death. After all, no one knew when Old Marshall had been born, and no one could be certain of the *exact* day on which he died.

The grave was tidied up, and Old Marshall was left in peace. A week later, Uncle Frank and Uncle Harry had been to town and were walking home.

They had left town in the afternoon, and before they got back, the sun went down and soon it was dark. They walked along teasing one another about being scared or not scared, and though Uncle Frank swore he was not scared of anything after what he had experienced at the MacReadie house, the truth was that he wished they were home and inside by now.

They were on the road just below the cemetery when Uncle Harry thought he heard something. Uncle Frank heard it too, but he wasn't going to admit to anything that might hold them up on the way home.

"Listen," Harry said. "It sounds like something scratching or digging."

He made Frank stop, and finally even Uncle Frank had to admit there was a loud digging, scratching sound coming from the direction of the cemetery.

"So you can hear it, too?" Uncle Harry asked.

"Of course I can hear it," Uncle Frank answered. "I've got ears, don't I?"

"Then if you can hear it and you're not scared of *anything*, how about going up there to see what it is. I'll wait right here for you."

After all the bragging he had done about being fearless, there was nothing Uncle Frank could do but pretend bravery, go up there, see what the source of the sound was, and get it over with. He puffed out his chest, told Harry he would be right back, and started up the cemetery hill toward the strange sound.

As soon as he was out of sight, Uncle Harry was not sure this had been such a good idea. He seemed to hear all kinds of new sounds as he waited, hoping his fearless brother would be back soon so they could both go home.

For his part, Uncle Frank was scared to death. As he entered the cemetery, the scudding clouds parted and the nearly full moon flooded the graveyard with chill light. There was something near the tall gravestone of Marshall MacReadie at the top of the hill.

As he crept closer, he hunched low to the ground to be less visible to anyone or anything there. He could hear the sound like someone scratching in the dirt on the other side of the tombstone from the direction of his approach. When he was about twenty yards away, he clearly saw a huge, dark cat sitting on top of the tombstone. Though he could still not see the source of the sound, he saw that the dark cat was looking around and around, as if it were standing lookout for the maker of the mysterious noise.

Uncle Frank crept closer. Suddenly he stepped on a rock that slipped under his foot and skittered away down the hillside.

At the sound, the dark cat spun on top of the gravestone and, with glowing eyes, looked straight at the frightened boy.

Uncle Frank searched the ground for a rock or stick to throw at the cat and, finding none, was filled with despair. Then he realized that his right shoe had come untied and was hanging loose on his foot. He stooped, removed the shoe, and drew back to fire it at the cat.

All at once the big cat stood up on its back feet, pointed one paw straight at Uncle Frank, and in a broguish voice unmistakable to his ears, screeched at him, *"Frank Davis, don't ye throw that thing et me!"*

Uncle Frank never knew what happened to the shoe. He just ran.

Harry heard him coming, but neither of them stopped to discuss anything. Anyone scared enough to run like this, Uncle Harry was thinking, had best not be asked why until he feels safe enough to want to tell you on his own.

In what seemed like moments, they burst through the door at home on the farm in Iron Duff and slammed and bolted it behind them.

Later on that night, as the whole family laughed at Uncle Frank for running all the way home with one shoe on and one shoe off, even Uncle Harry begin to pick at him for being so scared.

Uncle Frank's response to his brother came easily. "In the morning, Harry," he suggested, "you go back up there with me to look for my shoe!"

Granddaddy laughed. "That's a good idea, Frank. I think all of us ought to go." And so the plan was made.

After breakfast the next day, the entire family walked back up to the cemetery in search of Uncle Frank's abandoned shoe. When they arrived at the top of the graveyard hill, they saw a most curious sight.

Marshall MacReadie's gravestone was lying face down on the ground, nearly covering his fresh grave. The earth had been dug out from under the front edge until the huge stone had toppled, much as it had on the day he died. The words *Marshall MacReadie* were there for all the world to see, but the inscription *REST IN PEACE* was face down, pressed into the soil of the freshly filled grave, never to be seen again.

Neither Old Anna nor any of the black cats was ever seen in Iron Duff again.

# *Aunt Esther and the Missing Cats*

When my brother and I were boys, we loved to spend time at our Aunt Esther's house.

Aunt Esther was my daddy's little sister. She still is—she's now eighty-five years old—and I'm *still* scared of her.

Aunt Esther's was a fine place for two little boys to have great adventures.

Her house had a big attic. We would go with her up the stairs to the attic and watch while she searched for something or other she was certain she had put there. The attic was filled with trunks and boxes and broken toys and furniture and hanging clothes covered with sheets.

Aunt Esther would finally find the hatbox or roll of wrapping paper she was looking for, and we would come back down the stairs together. She'd lock the attic door and leave the key in the lock.

"Don't play in the attic, boys," she warned. "It's dusty and dirty up there, and there might be spiders."

There was a big basement at Aunt Esther's house. We had only a small cellar at home, so we were fascinated by this huge space with a full concrete floor and high windows to let the light in. The basement was lined with shelves for canned goods and stacked with boxes and baskets for storing potatoes and apples through the winter. There was a coal furnace and a small metal door through which the truck could dump coal into a walled-off bin Uncle Mark called "the stoker hole."

We would follow Aunt Esther into the basement in search of canned beans or apples. When we returned to the top of the stairs, she would latch the basement door with a screen-door hook.

"Don't play in the basement," she would say. "It's damp down there, and you might catch a cold, and there might be spiders!"

Aunt Esther and Uncle Mark had a garage in the back yard. In it lived their long, blue, nineteen-fifty-three Pontiac Super Chieftain, with the chrome stripes running down the hood and off the lid of the trunk. There was a wraparound sun visor and an amber-colored Indian-head ornament on the hood which lit up when the headlights were turned on at night.

We loved to ride in the Pontiac. The dome light came on even when you opened the *back* doors, and it had a heater under the front seat that blew warm air into the back.

We would come home from town, and Aunt Esther would have us get out before she parked the Pontiac in the narrow garage.

"Don't play in the garage, boys. You will get grease on your pants, and in that garage, there might be spiders!"

There was a woodshed on the back of the garage in which the Pontiac lived. Uncle Mark worked at a builders' supply house, and he brought home wood scraps from the cabinet shop so there would be dry wood to start fires in the stove in the wintertime.

We could see pieces of wood of every imaginable shape and size there in the woodshed. There were surely pieces in there perfect for building sleds and bird feeders and wagons.

"Don't play in the woodshed. First thing you know, you'll get splinters in your fingers, and there might be spiders in there!"

Aunt Esther had a much larger barn than ours. It had several stalls downstairs and a huge loft where hay bales were stacked.

From the loft, we could throw hay down into the mangers, and jump into them. We could go to the end of the loft, slide back the sliding door, and hook a bale of hay to the pulley-rope. Then we could throw the hooked bale to the ground, grab the other end of the rope, and ride the rope down while the hay bale rose to balance our weight.

"Don't play in the barn, boys. There is a big blacksnake that lives out there, and there might be spiders!"

People who only heard of Aunt Esther's prohibitions might wonder why two adventuresome boys would want to spend time there. The answer was simple.

Each morning when she finished washing the dishes, Aunt Esther headed out the kitchen door toward Mrs. Margaret Jones's house. At the same time, Mrs. Margaret Jones would finish washing her dishes and head out her back door toward Aunt Esther's house.

They would meet at the fence between the two yards and talk about *everybody.* They talked about who had done what and where and with whom and how often and why, until the grass was worn off on the ground under their feet.

While the two of them were out there handling everybody's business, my brother and I played—in the attic, in the basement, in the Pontiac, in the woodshed, in the barn...

What she doesn't know, we said, as boys will, won't hurt her!

One day, when Aunt Esther came back in from talking, she said, "Boys, let's kill a chicken and cook it for dinner."

That was just fine with us. We always had chickens at our house, and my brother and I often helped our Daddy kill and dress them.

We usually had Rhode Island Reds, and our Daddy was what you might call a "chopper." That is, he chopped the chickens' heads off in order to send them on their way to the frying pan.

We would go out to the hen house and get the victim. Daddy would pick one out, and we would all try to chase it down. The chase never worked out as planned, but somewhere along the way some luckless chicken would get tangled in the fence and make our next meal.

Daddy would carry the red hen back to the chopping block beside the woodshed.

I had a particular job at chicken killings. There was an old smokehouse, which we now used for storage, in the corner of the yard near the chopping block. The smokehouse was built on rock pilings and stood about a foot off the ground. My job was to stand between the chopping block and the smokehouse and, armed with a hoe handle or a tobacco stick, keep the chicken out from under the smokehouse.

Daddy would hold the chicken by the feet as he laid its neck on the chopping block. With a quick *whack*, he'd chop the Rhode Island Red's head right off and throw the rest of it on the ground where it could jump and flop for up to five minutes until it was completely dead.

Somehow, those headless, flopping chickens knew just which way to go to get under the smokehouse. I, with my stick, had to fight them back, like Errol Flynn in a pirate movie, so they would die in the open yard. (If I failed and they flopped under the smoke house, I would have to crawl back under there in the dirt and drag the dead hen out once it stopped flopping.)

My grandmother was not a chopper. She was a "wringer." When she wanted to kill a chicken she would wring its neck.

She had White Leghorns which she kept in a henhouse so that their eggs would be cleaner to sell. I'd see her emerge from the henhouse with the Leghorn under her arm. Without even putting it down, she would reach up with the same hand, surround its neck, and with a wind-up that would make a fast-pitch softball pitcher jealous, twist that chicken halfway to the frying pan! (On one Wednesday afternoon before Thanksgiving, I once saw her wring the necks of *two* hens at *one time,* one with each hand.)

The first time Aunt Esther said she wanted to kill a chicken and cook it for dinner, my brother and I both wondered at once whether she was a wringer or a chopper. There was no way to know but to wait and watch.

Before we went out to the chicken yard, Aunt Esther went into the kitchen. There she gathered the front of her apron to make a carrying pouch, and into it she scooped about a quart of chicken feed from its kitchen storage bin.

This seemed a bit strange to my brother and me. Why was she taking a treat to her chickens? She was supposed to be getting one to *kill.*

At the chicken yard, though, we began to see how smart she was. She dropped the chicken feed in a long stream on the ground, and when the chickens were eating, their heads down as if in prayer, all she had to do was pick up the fattest one. There was none of that chasing we had to do to get the Rhode Island Reds.

She had big, speckled, Dominecker hens. We watched as she picked up a fat one. She held a little bit of chicken feed in her hand, so that as she carried this hen under her arm, it could continue to eat and not even care it had been caught.

Without telling the rest of the hens what we were doing, and without giving this particular hen a chance to say good-bye to her sisters, we eased out the gate and left.

My brother was betting that Aunt Esther was a wringer, and he whispered to me, "If I'm right, it won't be long—she'll wring its neck before we're halfway back to the house."

It was not to be so. We followed Aunt Esther as she kept walking down through the pasture farther and farther from the chicken house. I just knew she was a chopper, and that we were surely headed for the woodshed chopping block.

We came to the woodshed and passed it right on by. By now, the chicken house was completely out of sight. We thought she had missed both of her best chances to dispatch this old hen.

I looked up at Aunt Esther and asked, "Why are we going so far down through here before you kill that chicken?"

She answered pleasantly, "Well, son, I don't want the rest of my chickens to see what it is that we are doing."

"Why?" my brother and I asked at once.

"Oh, boys," she smiled now, "it's like I've heard the two of you say: 'What they don't know won't hurt them!'"

Not realizing she had ever heard us say such a thing, the two of us felt our hearts leap.

By this time, the chicken had finished the feed in Aunt Esther's hand. She had grasped it by the feet and was carrying it, head down, swinging along with its wings laid back and its head barely brushing the top of the grass.

All of a sudden, without any warning in the world, Aunt Ester stepped on the chicken's head and gave its feet a sharp yank which snapped its head right off.

My brother looked at me with eyes the size of saucers. "She's a 'snapper'!" he cried out in amazement.

After that day, a great change came over the two of us boys. From then on, we paid a lot more attention to anything Aunt Esther told us, because we knew that when she meant business, she meant *business.*

After all else was said and done, the one thing we loved to do most of all at Aunt Esther's house was to play with her two old cats, Hair and Hambone.

Aunt Esther said that Hair was a blue cat. I tried to correct Aunt Esther and tell her that there were no blue animals, especially blue cats. Hair, I insisted, was gray.

Aunt Esther would not have this. "No," she insisted, "Hair is blue. She is exactly the color of old blue jeans which have been washed at least two thousand times!"

Hair was always there when we went to Aunt Esther's house, and with that long, blowing blue hair, I thought her to be the most beautiful cat in the world.

Hambone, on the other hand, was a commonly ugly gray tomcat.

Sometimes Hambone was at home when we were at Aunt Esther's house, and sometimes he was not.

"Where's Hambone?" I would ask Aunt Esther.

"Oh," she would answer, "Hambone's a tomcat, you know."

"So," I replied, "Where is he?"

"He's gone on a tour," Aunt Esther smugly replied. "He has a lot of girlfriends he's obliged to visit. He'll be back; don't worry."

And sure enough, late in the afternoon, Hambone would come dragging home. Aunt Esther would stand beside the back steps, put one foot up on the steps, slap her knee over and over again, and sing, "Hambone, Hambone, where you been? 'Around the world and I'm going again!'"

"Around the world!" I thought. "Why, that is amazing!" To me, "around the world" meant places like China and

Japan and Africa. No wonder that cat is so tired when he gets home, I thought. He's been everywhere!

One day we arrived at Aunt Esther's house early in the morning, ready to spend the entire day. As soon as breakfast was over, we began to look for Hair and Hambone while Aunt Esther washed the dishes. We couldn't find either one of the cats.

This was strange. Hambone was often missing, but Hair was *always* at home. Something funny was going on here. We better check this out.

My brother and I waited until Aunt Esther had finished the dishes and was out at the fence talking with Margaret Jones. Then we went into action.

We searched the attic, we looked in the basement, we checked the Pontiac, we examined the woodshed, we went all over the barn. We found a thousand spiders, but the two cats were simply no place to be found.

My brother asked, "What do we do now?"

"I don't know," I replied, then added, "I guess we'll just have to ask Aunt Esther."

The last place we had searched for the two cats was at the barn, and so we now walked back down through the pasture, past the chicken lot, and toward Aunt Esther's house. We could see that she was no longer at the "talking fence," but we didn't see her anywhere else. She must be inside the house.

There was a little picket fence around the back yard, and the gate to the fence opened into the yard just under a big grape arbor Uncle Mark had built there. The arbor was built of pipes and fence wire and had a big post right in the middle which the grapevines climbed before they spread out on top. This was the one shady place in the back yard, and the place where Aunt Esther and Uncle Mark had several white, wooden lawn chairs.

We came in the gate and under the grapevines when suddenly we spotted Aunt Esther. She was coming around the side of the house, dusting her hands off against one another. Uncle Mark was about ten yards behind her, carrying a shovel.

When they saw us, he tried to hide the shovel behind his back and began to back out of sight around the corner of the house. She, however, just called, "Hello, boys!" and came up to meet us at the grape vines.

My brother asked the question for both of us. "Aunt Esther, we can't find Hair and we can't find Hambone...can you tell us what might have happened to them?"

Without a moment's hesitation she replied, "Of course I can." Then she took the two of us to a wide, double lawn chair, sat down in the center of it, and squeezed one of us on each side of her.

"Let me ask you a question to begin with, boys," she started. "What do cats like to eat?"

"Mice!" I was first to guess.

"That's right." Before I had a chance to feel good about the correct answer, she asked, "What else?"

This time my brother answered, "Fish?" with a little more hesitation.

"That's right too!" she quickly chimed. "What else?"

For the next few minutes, the two of us guessed every food we could possibly think of that cats might eat. Her response was always the same.

"Cat food!"

"That's right. What else?"

"Hamburger!"

"Milk!"

"Liver!"

"Green beans!"

No matter what we guessed, it was always right—but somehow not enough. "What else?" she would ask.

Finally we were guessed out. We had named every food we had ever heard of and still we were missing something.

"You've done a good job guessing, boys. A very good job. But you have failed to name the one thing in the world cats would rather eat than anything else."

"*What is it?*" both of us asked in loud and determined unison.

Looking straight up over our heads, Aunt Esther pointed into the grape vines and said, "Grapes!"

Neither my brother nor I had ever heard of such a thing. We were astounded.

"Yes, boys," she went on, "cats would rather eat grapes than anything else in the world.

"Why, many times I have looked out the kitchen window while washing dishes and seen Hair and Hambone come out here to get some grapes. They climb this post here in the middle, pick a bunch of ripe grapes, lean back and cross their legs, peel those grapes and pick the seeds out with their claws, and eat them a bite at a time. If they're in a big hurry, they pop the entire grape in their mouths, spit out the hull, and swallow the rest whole.

"Cats love grapes!"

Well, now we knew, believe it or not. "What does this have to do with what happened to Hair and Hambone?" My brother asked the question I was thinking.

"Just listen a minute, and I'll make that clear to both of you."

We listened intently.

"It was yesterday afternoon, boys," she began the story. "I was in the kitchen beginning to fix supper.

"As I glanced out the window, I saw Hair and Hambone come around through here and start to climb that post to get up there and get some grapes to eat. When they were about halfway up the post, it happened: Hair looked up and saw a big blacksnake up there in the grapevines. It had crawled up to try to catch a bird when the birds come to peck at those ripe grapes.

"Hair pointed to the snake, and Hambone nodded. It was clear to both of them that they would not get any grapes today with that snake there. They both climbed down from the post."

She paused a little too long for me. "Then what happened?" I asked.

"Well, just as they got almost out from under the grapevines, Hambone stood up, turned to Hair, and said, 'Hair, in all my travels around the world, I think I may have learned a way we can get up there and get some grapes without having to climb past that snake to do it.'

"Hair asked how, and Hambone explained it to her.

"'You just climb on my back and we can do it,' Hambone instructed Hair.

"'That won't work,' Hair replied. 'You're not tall enough. We still won't be able to reach them.'

"'Just do what I tell you,' Hambone insisted.

"Then, boys, Hambone hunkered down on the ground while Hair climbed onto his back. When she was up there, he continued his instructions. 'Now, Hair, pull in your front legs, and pull in your back legs and take a big breath, and don't move a muscle. Be just as still as you can,' he said.

"Now, boys, pay attention to this part. When Hair was completely still all over, Hambone slipped out from under her. She was holding so still that she *didn't move,* but sat there, about four inches off of the ground, *right in the air!*

"Then," she continued as we listened intently, "Hambone climbed right on up on her back!

"When he was as still as he could be, he said to her, 'Now climb up here on top of me.' Hair did what she was told, and now they were about eight inches off the ground, right there in the air!"

"Did they keep doing that?" I asked.

"They surely did," she answered. "It was Hair on Hambone, Hambone on Hair, back and forth, over and over. I watched the two of them climb right through the air and up toward those grapevines, but..."

(Somehow I knew that this was too good to go on.)

"Boys, they were doing so well, that... well, I think they just forgot where they were going, and they passed those grapes and went right on by, still climbing on one another's backs.

"The last thing I saw yesterday afternoon, boys, was Hair and Hambone just getting smaller and smaller and smaller and fading out of sight way up there in the sky."

"What happened to them?" I would not have asked another question, but my brother did.

Aunt Esther answered with a question of her own: "What is the moon made out of?"

"Green cheese!" we answered together. We both knew that.

"That is correct, boys, and that is the key to the answer.

"What I think is that by the time Hair and Hambone realized how high they were, it was too late to come back, and so they just went on to the moon. I think they are living there now, boys, eating the rats and mice that are eating away at that green-cheese moon!"

With that, she left us sitting under the grapevines and headed off to the house.

Uncle Mark was there by the back door. He was still holding the shovel behind his back, and he had been listening to her story.

As Aunt Esther passed him on her way in the door, he asked her gruffly, "Aw, Esther, what did you tell them that for?"

Her reply came quickly, "Because, Mark, what they don't know won't hurt them!"

# Uncle Gudger's First Pet

*U*ncle Gudger grew up alongside Cataloochee Creek way up in the northernmost part of the Haywood County mountains. Nobody lives up there anymore because the old Cataloochee community is part of the Great Smoky Mountains National Park now, but back when Uncle Gudger was a child, a lot of families did.

There was a school and a church and quite a sizable population living alongside Cataloochee Creek for many generations.

Uncle Gudger and his mother lived in a big house across Cataloochee Creek from the road that ran through the middle of the valley. In order to get anywhere from the house, you had to cross the creek on a footlog, a narrow bridge made by planing one side of a log flat with an adze and then setting it across the creek with the flat side up.

Every morning when school was in session, Uncle Gudger had to cross the creek on the footlog in order to get to the road and walk his way on up to the schoolhouse.

Uncle Gudger never did mind going to school, but he did have a bit of trouble with some of what was involved in getting ready for it every day.

It seems that his mother had gotten so used to cooking for a big household of people that even when everybody but Gudger was grown and gone, she just kept right on cooking the same old way. This profusion of food, together with her idea that "you have to be good and stout when you grow up in order to take care of yourself," made eating breakfast a great chore for my Uncle Gudger.

He would get up, get all dressed and ready for school, and then face a table full of vittles sufficient to feed at least a half-dozen people. He would eat and eat and eat, and still his mother never thought he ate enough to make him "good and stout" the way she wanted him to be.

"Make all that food disappear, Gudger," she would say as he struggled to comply.

Then one day, Uncle Gudger had a thought. "It was a revelation out of nowhere," he said when he was called upon much later to tell about it.

"I was still in bed," he said, "not even quite all the way awake yet, when I heard this voice. It whispered to me, 'Gudger...Gudger...she never said you have to *eat* all of that food!'

"Why, I sat right up in bed. The voice was absolutely right. All she had ever said was, 'Make that food *disappear.*' I knew right then there must be a lot of different ways you could make food disappear."

Prompted by his "revelation," Uncle Gudger soon devised a new method of eating breakfast.

Holding a biscuit in his hand, he would take a big mouthful of eggs and watch his mother carefully. As soon as she glanced away from him, he would spit the egg into the split biscuit and stuff the biscuit far out of sight down in the bib of his overalls.

In less than a half an hour, all the food on the table had "disappeared," and Mrs. Palmer was mightily pleased.

"You will be good and stout in no time!" she proudly told him. Uncle Gudger smiled and tried not to let any of the food fall out of the side of his overall bib.

The only problem left was what to do with the food once he had made it out of the house.

He fairly waddled down the path to Cataloochee Creek while he pondered his dilemma. He though to himself, "I could just let down my overall flap and dump it here on the ground and hope a dog or something would come along and eat it before Mama sees it... but... if she should find out I've not eaten all this food, I'll be in bad trouble for sure!"

Uncle Gudger was walking while he thought, and by now, he was crossing the footlog over the creek, still thinking and thinking of how to dispose of what he had already made disappear.

As he passed over the creek on the footlog, a loose biscuit slipped from its safe place and rolled down the leg of his overalls. The biscuit bounced on the footlog, dropped down into the creek, and sank out of sight.

"This is the answer!" Uncle Gudger thought. "I will shake all this food down my britches leg and into the creek, and the evidence will just wash away!" And so he did.

The result, however, was even better than he expected. As soon as the food hit the water, fish began to appear from everywhere, drawn by the splashing and by the good smell of Mrs. Palmer's cooking. A whole community of trout had a hearty breakfast off Uncle Gudger's leavings.

"Look at that!" he said to himself. "Look at those fish! I'll feed these fish every day, and then when I want to catch one, they will be right here waiting for me. That's what I will do."

From that day on, breakfast food disappeared faster than ever in the Palmer house. The fish were well fed, Uncle Gudger was greatly relieved, and Mrs. Palmer was happy that her little boy was surely going to grow up to be good and stout like she had always hoped he would be.

Several weeks later, something unexpected happened at the footlog.

Uncle Gudger was on his way to school with his overall bib stashed full of food for the fish. They usually listened for the sound of his footsteps on the footlog and gathered in an instant for their feeding.

On this morning, though, there were no fish to be seen. Uncle Gudger walked out to the middle of the footlog and looked down. "Where are my fish?" he wondered aloud to himself. "Have they all overslept? Did somebody catch them all in the night? Did it rain real hard and wash them away?"

The fish were in such a habit of being there; he couldn't figure it out.

Suddenly he saw movement in the water. Something was swimming slowly out from a hiding place beneath a log beside the creek bank. Uncle Gudger watched to see what it was and wondered whether it might have something to do with his missing trout.

When it got close enough, he saw that it was a huge, brown fish with a broad mouth and long whiskers!

He didn't know what a catfish was. No one had ever seen a catfish in Cataloochee Creek before. This one must have spotted a few crumbs of missed biscuit which had washed all the way down to the Tennessee River. The big Tennessee River catfish must have followed the trail of crumbs up Tennessee, up the French Broad, up the Pigeon River, and finally, back up the Cataloochee Creek, where it was looking for the source of the free breakfast.

He didn't know if the big catfish had chased all the trout away so it could have the food to itself, or if the astonished trout had taken off on their own. Why, this fish looked like it weighed twenty-five or thirty pounds if it weighed an ounce.

It made Uncle Gudger mad to think that this big outlander of a fish might be such a selfish bully that all of his regular diners had been scared away from their natural home feeding ground. He took a big heavy biscuit out of his overalls, drew back, and threw it like a rock at the whiskered fish.

That biscuit never even got wet! The big catfish rolled over on his back, gave a big push out of the water, and caught that biscuit right in the air like a center fielder. Uncle Gudger watched as the fish settled down in the water, chewing and grinning.

He might have to reconsider his feelings about this intruder. After all, none of the trout he had been feeding put on such a show. Maybe this was a fish worth feeding!

Uncle Gudger was late to school that day. He spent most of an hour playing catch with that catfish. The fish could catch biscuits, fried eggs, squares of cornbread, and even grits (if they were shaped and thrown like a snowball).

"This *is* a fish worth feeding," he said to himself.

From that day on, fish feeding was more fun than ever. Each morning, he would gather the meal with care, considering the kinds of breakfast items that would be easiest or most interesting for the big fish to catch.

He was making so much food disappear that Mrs Palmer didn't understand why he wasn't getting any stouter than he was. She figured he ought to weigh about a hundred and fifty pounds by now, but he seemed to look just about the same as before. It was a mystery.

After a few days of feeding, the catfish came to be considered by Uncle Gudger a personal pet. A pet ought to have a name, he thought. He spent several days considering appropriate names for a catfish which was fast becoming a member of his personal family.

Every name Uncle Gudger had ever heard, he had heard because it belonged to someone who lived on Cataloochee.

He had simply never been anywhere to hear any other names. Every time he considered a name for the catfish, it didn't seem right to use because it also belonged to a relative or a neighbor.

"I don't want," thought Uncle Gudger considerately, "to offend any of my neighbors or kinfolks by having them think I named a fish after them!"

And so, after much consideration, Uncle Gudger decided to name the fish "Haywood County," after the county in which they lived, and since that was such a long name, he would call it "H.C." for short.

If the catfish had a sizeable ego before he was named, he outshone himself now that he had a name given him by a human. He would be waiting each morning, without any patience whatsoever, for Uncle Gudger to feed him. On top of that, H.C. began to expect to be fed every afternoon, too.

As Uncle Gudger walked home from school, there would be the big fish, swimming around and sticking his head out of the water to fuss. Finally, the boy started packing two lunches for school. He would save one for H.C. and feed the catfish on his own way home each afternoon.

This daily routine continued on through the fall of the year as school wended its slow course toward winter.

With the days growing shorter and the weather cooling off, Uncle Gudger and his friends often took advantage of the warmer days to play for a while after school before they went home for the day. After all, when the deep cold of winter came, there would be neither time nor weather for play until the spring.

On these days, Uncle Gudger would be late coming home, and Haywood County Catfish would be angry and impatient waiting for his afternoon feeding. The big fish would stick his head out of the water and fuss for a few minutes before he would ever settle down and eat. This was a fish who knew how to get his way.

One especially pretty day, the big catfish was so mad because Uncle Gudger was late that he had hauled himself out of the water and was sitting on the creek bank waiting when his feeder finally came dragging home. H.C. actually shook his fin at Uncle Gudger and fussed for a full five minutes before he would consent to be fed.

Uncle Gudger walked down the creek bank where the angry fish was seated. He pulled a jelly-biscuit from the lunch bucket and extended it as a peace offering to the catfish. H.C. ate the jelly-biscuit right out of the boy's hand!

While it ate, Uncle Gudger began to pet the fish, to scratch it gently behind the gills, to stroke its belly.

The big catfish had never been petted before, and he loved it! He did everything but purr to get Uncle Gudger to keep going and not stop. H.C. had discovered the wonder of affectionate human touch!

The next day, there he was again, right up there on the bank. He was not fussing now but purring and begging to be petted. Uncle Gudger offered him an egg sandwich and watched H.C. eat it. The boy petted and spoiled him some more.

When the fish had finished eating, Uncle Gudger told him goodbye and headed for home. After he had gone a few steps, he heard strange sounds coming from behind him. They were a whining cry and a flop–flop noise.

When he turned around, he saw H.C. The big fish was crying after him and trying to follow him home. Uncle Gudger shooed the fish back into the creek, laughed to himself, and continued on home.

From that day on, H.C. was determined to follow Uncle Gudger home. Every day, the boy would have to chase his pet back into the water before going home to get his own supper.

One day Mrs. Palmer asked him, "Gudger, why have you been getting later and later in coming home from school?"

Uncle Gudger decided to tell the truth and have it over with.

"Well, Mama," he began his answer cautiously, "I have a big pet catfish down there in the creek."

"Sure you do, Gudger." She almost laughed at him. "Why don't you tell me the truth?"

"I'm telling you the truth Mama," he insisted. "His name is 'Haywood County,' and every day he comes out of the water and I play with him. Why, he's even been trying to follow me home!"

"Sure he has, Gudger. Why don't you just bring him on up here and introduce him to me?"

Mrs. Palmer, who thought she would uncover a made-up story, was fairly well shocked the next afternoon when Uncle Gudger and Haywood County Catfish came up the trail to the house walking hand in fin. The big fish, now bigger than ever, walked along on his tail and jumped up the front steps one at a time in order to get on the porch and into the house itself.

Mrs. Palmer was so taken aback that she didn't even object as Gudger took H.C. inside and showed him all around the house.

The two of them played upstairs and downstairs all through the afternoon and on into the evening. Once in a while, H.C. would get out of breath, and Uncle Gudger would help him stick his head in a bucket of drinking water.

After that day, Uncle Gudger started bringing Haywood County home with him on the weekends. The fish was soon housebroken so that it used a sandbox just like a housecat would, and then it moved from sleeping on a wet towel in the kitchen to sleeping right in the featherbed with

Uncle Gudger himself. It seemed to him that H.C. had truly become a member of the family.

The pattern of weekend visitation continued on into the winter.

One weekend when H.C. was at home with the Palmers, the hard cold of deep winter descended over Cataloochee. The temperature dropped to well below freezing, and it was difficult to keep warm even in the house with a big fire in the woodstove.

On Monday morning when, as was his habit, Uncle Gudger went to return H.C. to the creek on his way to school, he found that in the cold of the weekend all of Cataloochee Creek had frozen over. The catfish could not get back into the water, and so he stayed to winter over with the Palmers.

Uncle Gudger loved this. He had never had a pet before, and the experience of having H.C. in the house with him was more than he could ever have hoped for.

The two of them played all the time when Uncle Gudger was home from school. They were inseparable. Why, when he did his homework, Uncle Gudger would read to H.C. out of the geography book, and he actually taught the fish a little bit of arithmetic. (H.C. would slap his fins on the table to indicate the answer to addition and subtraction problems.)

Finally springtime came.

The air was fresh and full of fresh new life, and Mrs. Palmer was ready to open all the windows and do her spring cleaning.

"It's time for that fish to go back to the creek, Gudger," she insisted. "This house is getting a peculiar odor I don't exactly care for. I'm not sure I want any of the neighbors dropping in until I can de-fishify this place."

Uncle Gudger begged, but there was no deal to be made. He could continue to play with Haywood County outdoors, but at least through the hot weather, the catfish could not stay in the house.

Uncle Gudger did get H.C.'s residency extended for one last weekend, and when that was over, the Monday morning trip to school was also to be the trip back to Cataloochee Creek for Haywood County.

Uncle Gudger was as slow as could be on that Monday morning. He slowly packed a lunch for H.C. and himself, and the two of them went slowly on their way down from the house.

As they neared Cataloochee Creek, Uncle Gudger thought maybe the fish would be glad to get back to his natural home. As reluctant to leave Uncle Gudger as Uncle Gudger was for him to go, the catfish hopped slowly along the footlog. He seemed intent on following Uncle Gudger right on to school.

"Oh, no!" Uncle Gudger thought, "this is Mary and her little lamb all over again!"

He was about halfway across the footlog when it happened. The footlog was still wet and slippery with the dew. Though Uncle Gudger knew how to watch his step, H. C. did not.

Suddenly, the big pet stepped on a slick spot, and his tailfin flew out from under him. He fell right off that footlog head first into the deep waters of Cataloochee Creek.

Uncle Gudger broke into a run and tore off the far end of the footlog and down to the edge of the creek. He was too late. Haywood County Catfish had stayed out of the water so long that he had forgotten how to swim, and the big fish drowned right there in the creek from which he had come.

And that was the sad and tragic end of Uncle Gudger's first pet.

# How To Get Rid of an Overfed Cat

*T*hings were very sad at Uncle Gudger's house following the tragic and untimely death of Haywood County. This catfish had, after all, been Uncle Gudger's very first pet, and he had grown quite attached to it.

He moped around the house and remembered all the adventures he'd had with H.C. He fell off in his ability to make food disappear, as there seemed to be little reason to do so anymore.

His mother took to calling the footlog where the tragedy had occurred the "Bridge of Sighs," because Uncle Gudger just sighed and sighed every time he had to cross it.

After several weeks of mourning, Uncle Gudger came to his mother one morning and started talking.

"Mama," he began, "I do miss Haywood County, but I know that I can't just go around for the rest of my life whimpering and crying. It's time for life to go on. And I want another pet to help me get my mind off old H.C."

That seemed fair enough, and his mama told him so. She asked him just exactly what he might have in mind.

"I don't want another fish, Mama," he answered. "I think it would be better if I got either a dog or a cat. Yes, ma'am, a dog or a cat ought to make me feel a whole lot better. Can I have a dog or a cat?"

"No dogs!" she snapped. "I simply am not going to have some kind of little yap-yap-excuse-for-a-dog running all over this house, sliding his toenails and scratching everything all up...because you *would* want it in the house after getting used to having that fish in here!

"Gudger, I'll tell you what. I wouldn't mind if you got yourself a nice, calm, quiet cat. Cats can at least do a little toward earning their keep." Then she asked, "What do you think about that?"

Uncle Gudger was overjoyed. He could hardly believe it. He actually had permission to get himself a cat—and, along with permission, the sure and certain knowledge that the cat would, in fact, eventually be allowed to live in the house.

As he tells the story, it wasn't easy to find a cat in Cataloochee. There were no telephones, and communication was quite slow. In fact, it took nearly twenty minutes for Uncle Gudger to locate a family with kittens to give away.

The cat donors were a family of Hannahs, and the word was that they had five kittens ready to go to good homes.

Uncle Gudger and Mrs. Palmer headed for the Hannahs' house. By the time they arrived, four of the kittens had already been adopted. Only the runt remained.

This poor kitten was so tiny it would fit in a good-sized teacup. It had little tiny ears and little tiny feet and a short tail that looked like the sharpened-down stub of a used-up pencil. It was gray and mottled-looking all over.

Uncle Gudger's mama just looked at it. The Hannahs didn't say anything—the little runt cat had already been turned down by three prospective owners.

Uncle Gudger thought the tiny cat was beautiful! The Hannahs were relieved! Mrs. Palmer was uncertain but happy!

And so Uncle Gudger had a new pet.

The little cat, having been pushed out of the trough by her bigger brothers and sisters, had never really had enough to eat. It seemed to be starved to death. When Uncle Gudger gave it a bowl of leftover chicken dressing and gravy, the cat ate it faster than a tenth grader and started meowing for more!

Uncle Gudger was thrilled. So, he fed the cat again. He discovered that he and the cat were made for one another. He loved the attention he got when the cat begged for food, and the cat loved the food!

"Don't feed that cat too much, Gudger," his mama said. "If you feed anything too much, you won't ever be able to get rid of it!"

Her warning reminded Uncle Gudger he hadn't fed the little cat for a few minutes, and so he fed it again right then. The truth was he didn't want to ever think about having to get rid of this new pet, and so if feeding made it hard to get rid of, he would feed it as often as he could.

Now that it had its chance, the little cat was a natural eater. It could and would eat anything Uncle Gudger came up with for it. It was out to make up for all the times it had been crowded out of the chow line when it was still the runt of the litter.

As the cat ate, the cat began to grow. And when it grew, it *grew!* Before long, no one in Cataloochee had ever seen a cat the size of this one. Why, tourists would stop their cars and take pictures whenever they saw the big critter. If Uncle Gudger was around, they would always ask, "What kind of animal is that? Is that a tame mountain lion or something?"

In the natural progression of pet bonding, Uncle Gudger soon realized the cat needed a name, just as

Haywood County Catfish had. This time, he had a plan to find a good and proper name for the new family member.

The naming plan was this: since the cat loved to eat so much, Uncle Gudger decided to name it for the food it liked to eat more than anything else in the world.

This process took a while. In the late summer, it looked like the cat's name might be "Squash" or "Fish Innards." Up in the fall of the year, it looked like "Pumpkin," or later, "Turkey," might be its natural handle.

Finally, however, when all was carefully observed over a period of about six months, the cat was named "Livermush." Though it would eat anything put before it, its favorite food in the entire world was a good leftover plate of fried livermush. That cat could put down livermush like nobody's business!

Livermush got bigger and bigger. The bigger she got the more she could eat, and the more she ate the bigger she got. She looked bigger than any of Uncle Gudger's first-grade classmates. He decided he would find out how much Livermush weighed.

The following Saturday, he put a mule halter on Livermush and led her (not without difficulty) down to the office of the logging railroad. He knew they had a big weight-balance scale there that they would let him use to weigh the cat.

He and a couple of the logging men put the cat on the scales and began to put more weights on the balance arm.

When the scale finally came to rest, the three of them looked at one another—and at Livermush—in horror and astonishment. She weighed fifty-six pounds and didn't appear to have her growth yet!

Now Uncle Gudger knew why Livermush looked bigger than the first graders. There was not actually one student in the first grade at Cataloochee School who weighed fifty-six pounds. This cat was a champion all the way around!

Back home at the Palmer house, there was a problem developing with Mrs. Palmer and the big cat.

Whenever she got her churn and filled it up with cream to make butter, she had to be careful not to look away for a second. If she did, Livermush would rare up on the churn and lean down inside to lap up some cream. Once, the whole churn turned over, and more than a gallon of thick cream ran all over the kitchen. Mrs. Palmer had to churn in the closet for safety reasons.

Then there were the featherbeds. That cat liked to climb up on the featherbeds and run around under the covers. With claws the size of eight-penny nails, she ripped the ticks to pieces and feathers went everywhere! It was like walking into a snowstorm.

Finally there was the terrible effect of those giant cat claws on the hardwood floors, which were not hard enough. Whenever Livermush slid to a stop with claws extended, shavings curled up from a floor which would never be smooth again.

All in all, Livermush was turning the house into a disaster area.

"Gudger," his mama said with great seriousness, "we have got to get rid of this cat. It is simply ruining our dwelling place."

"But she's my pet," he whimpered. "Can't we give her another chance?"

Mrs. Palmer was lenient with the chances, but in the end, the damage was so extensive that the two of them decided together to try to find Livermush a new home.

The Hannah family who had given the cat to them in the first place thought they would try to take her back. It seems one of their mules had died, and they thought they might break Livermush and train her to plow.

They did hitch the cat to a hillside plow and tried her out for a round, but when they were switching the plow at the end of the row, she bolted. Livermush climbed a big oak tree, plow and all. Then she got the lines all tangled up in the tree limbs, wiggled around until *she* was loose, and came back down out of the tree, leaving the hillside plow up there forever.

The Hannahs sent Livermush back home.

A little bit later, a man who had a store in Cosby, Tennessee, thought he might try Livermush out as a watchcat. It seemed he was having a lot of trouble with break-ins and theft, and since the cat wouldn't bark and scare the culprits off before he could catch them, she might be the perfect solution.

Livermush spent one night in the store before being sent back home. Everything which was not canned—boxed food, bagged food, packaged food, loose food—everything was eaten by Livermush in one night.

The store owner declared he could leave the doors unlocked and end up in better shape than if he had any more help from that cat.

Several times, Uncle Gudger hauled her way off into the mountains and just dumped her. He was sure Livermush could take care of herself. She could. She was always back home before he could get back there in horse and wagon.

The house was being destroyed and it seemed hopeless. Mrs. Palmer was finally at the very end of her rope.

"Gudger," she said one day, "you are just going to have to shoot that cat. It has got to go!"

In spite of her destructiveness, Uncle Gudger really did not want to shoot his Livermush. Then one day something happened to convince him he might have to do just that.

It was springtime now, and as was her usual habit, Mrs. Palmer was doing her thorough spring housecleaning.

All the furniture had been moved out on the porch, and the floors had been scrubbed. The feather mattresses were put outside to air, and all the bedding was washed and hung out. All the curtains in the house were washed and spread over bushes in the yard to dry.

Livermush watched all these goings-on with feline curiosity. She had never noticed so many separate interesting items from the house until they were moved out of place.

She paid attention to Uncle Gudger and his mother as they started rehanging the curtains, especially the big double-rodded set on the front windows in the living room.

It looked to Livermush as though it might be quite fine to climb to the tops of these curtains and establish a lookout—from the rods, she could look down on the entire living-room world!

Livermush was smart enough not to try anything funny while Mrs. Palmer and Uncle Gudger were in the room. No, she waited until it was all clear before she tried what she was thinking of.

While Uncle Gudger and his mother were folding bed-linens in the kitchen, and nobody was watching, Livermush extended her eight-penny cat claws and started climbing to the tops of those freshly washed living-room curtains.

The big cat got all the way to the top of the curtains before anything happened, and then everything broke loose at once. The claw-hold no longer held, and to hear Uncle Gudger tell about it later, "it sounded like there were ten or twelve men in the living room all zipping their pants up and down, up and down, at the same time. We ran in there to see what was the matter. What we saw was Mama's fresh-washed window curtains hanging in ribbons!"

"Gudger," Mrs. Palmer said, "I want you to *shoot* that cat. I just can't stand it anymore!"

By this time, Uncle Gudger had to agree. There was simply nothing left to do.

He took Livermush above the barn and shot her. Then he buried her in a hole he had dug beside the garden. Their troubles were over now.

But three days later, Livermush was back at home, just licking her paws and washing the dirt off of herself. It had taken her the three days to dig herself up, or she would have been back sooner.

Uncle Gudger couldn't believe it, but he did see it! What were they going to do now?

Then the truth hit him. He knew exactly what the problem was *and* how to solve it. It was so simple. He had heard it all his life without realizing how important a thing it was to know.

He repeated the just-discovered truth to himself. "Cats have nine lives! Cats have *nine* lives, and to get rid of a cat the likes of Livermush, you must have to kill it at least nine times at once, and kill every bit of it!

Uncle Gudger set to work. It took him nine days to make his plans and gather his equipment.

He retrieved his daddy's pistol from its storage place in the chest of drawers and secured nine bullets for it. He sharpened up his mother's nine-inch-long butcher knife. He spent nine hours digging a hole nine feet deep in the edge of the woods above the garden. After that, he went through the barn until he had found nine tow sacks and nine good, strong pieces of tow string. Lastly, he scratched and scraped through the garden until he had gathered nine big rocks, each one of which was the size of a grown man's head.

At last he was ready. He took the big cat up into the woods and shot it nine times, straight through the head. The cat fell down and seemed to be dead.

"Now I've killed the part that thinks," he said to himself aloud. "The next thing is to kill the part that works."

He took the butcher knife with the nine-inch blade and cut the cat's head off. Then he buried the head in the hole he had dug nine feet deep in the ground.

"You stay down there!" he yelled down into the hole, just before filling it up. "You don't have any way to dig yourself out now, do you?"

Next Uncle Gudger took the rest of the cat, "the working part," he had called it. He put this part of the cat in a tow sack, added a rock to the sack, and tied it with one of the pieces of string.

Then he put this load into another sack, added another rock, and, of course, tied it with another piece of string. This process went on until the working part of the cat had been placed inside nine sacks weighted down with nine rocks and tied with all nine of the pieces of the string.

He now dragged this awful load down to the "Bridge of Sighs," pulling it behind him as he made his way out to the middle of the footlog, and dropped it into Cataloochee Creek.

He watched with genuinely mixed emotions as he saw the weighted sack sink to the bottom, then bounce its way down along the rocks on the bed of the creek.

It was over at last.

Uncle Gudger and his mama waited cautiously for three days. This was the longest that Livermush had ever been gone. The cat did not come back.

They waited for a full week. Still all was quiet and catless. They thought that surely they were safe.

Mrs. Palmer brought her churn out of the closet and churned right in the middle of the kitchen floor! She mended all of the feather mattresses and made up the beds freshly.

Finally, she ordered herself a new set of living room curtains from the Sears and Roebuck catalogue. All was going to be normal again after all.

And then...

When he told about it much later, Uncle Gudger says it was nine days from the time they had started counting. It was probably about nine o'clock in the morning, because, he said, he had eaten nine pancakes for breakfast, and that takes some time to do.

Uncle Gudger and his mama heard a noise outside in the front yard.

"Open the door, Gudger," she said. "See what's making that racket."

"If you want it open, Mama," he replied with wide eyes, "you're just going to have to open it yourself. I don't care what's out there, and I don't need to look at it."

Still, he could not keep from watching as his mother went to the front door of the house and opened the door.

There in the front yard, not *nine* feet from the front porch of the house, covered with dirt and at the same time dripping wet...there stood Livermush, holding her head in her mouth!

"I told you, Gudger," Mrs. Palmer was shaking her finger at him, "that if you feed anything too much, you won't *ever* be able to get rid of it!"

# Old Man Hawkins's Lucky Day

*T*he road from town to Iron Duff ran alongside the Pigeon River, which at one point passed through Bowlegged Valley. As we traveled that portion of the road on the way to Uncle Frank's house, we would often look across the river and be reminded of the log house where Old Man Hawkins once lived. When we asked, Daddy would once again tell us the remarkable story of Old Man Hawkins's lucky day of hunting in the woods along the Pigeon River.

Nobody ever heard what the rest of Old Man Hawkins's actual name was. His wife just called him "Old Man," and then his children called him "Old Man," all the neighbors called him "Old Man," and whatever his given name was (if he had one) was long since forgotten.

Being located above the river and having a front porch which overlooked the Bowlegged Valley, Old Man Hawkins's house was a frequent place for community meetings, visitation, and above all, gossip.

Most people enjoyed stopping to sit on the porch and visit, but even the most inveterate talker would finally grow tired of Old Man Hawkins's single subject of perpetual conversation. He could simply not be stopped from bragging that he was the greatest hunter in all of Haywood County, perhaps even the greatest hunter in all the world!

"When I go hunting," he would firmly declare, "I always like to take a mirror with me."

His neighbors would laugh and say, "How come? Do you want to comb your hair out there in the woods?"

"Of course not," he would answer. "What I do is walk right on past animals that are hiding from me, and then, when they think I am gone, I look in that mirror, aim back over my shoulder, and shoot things that don't even know I'm looking at them! What do you think of that?"

Everyone would laugh and wait to hear whatever it was Old Man Hawkins would come up with next.

"When I go squirrel hunting, I always take a twenty-two rifle and a double-bitted axe!"

"What do you need with the axe?" one of his listeners asked. "You don't have to cut the tree down to get a squirrel out of it."

"I know that," Old Man Hawkins said. "I take the axe up in the woods, though, and chop it way up into the side of a tree. Then I get down the hill a good distance below that.

"When I'm ready, I shoot the blade of the axe, split the twenty-two bullet, and kill *two* squirrels at once every time!"

This feat left everyone speechless, so, Old Man Hawkins was free to continue.

"What I *really* like to do is to go deer hunting when a hard wind is blowing."

"Why?" all of his neighbors asked in unison. He had lost them completely with this one.

"Well, its like this," he filled them in. "I take a muzzle loader and spit on the bullet before I load it up. Then I can shoot a curving spit-bullet across that wind and hit a deer that doesn't even know that I'm shooting at it at all. It works every time."

One of his neighbors piped up. "Why don't you go hunting with us and show us how it is you do all these things?"

Old Man Hawkins was quick to answer. "Why, fellers, if I went, I'd kill everything! There wouldn't be anything left to shoot at at all after I got finished. No, I better just stay here on the porch and let you go."

The *truth* is Old Man Hawkins had never been hunting in his life! He had never owned a gun; he had never shot a gun; he didn't even know how to *load* a gun.

When he was a little boy, he had started telling these big hunting tales, and as he got bigger and older, his tales got bigger along with him. He wouldn't have any idea what to do if he had to go hunting, but nobody else knew this.

Finally, three of his neighbors got tired of listening to him brag without ever seeing the proof of all his talk. They came up with a plan to force Old Man Hawkins to do it or shut up. After talking it over, they showed up at his house one Sunday afternoon to explain what they had in mind.

"Old Man," the spokesman began, "those of us who live around here are beginning to get a little bit tired of all this talk of yours. I mean, we want to see if you can really do any of the stuff you keep bragging about. This is what we're going to do. Next Saturday you *are* going to go hunting, like it or not."

Old Man Hawkins just listened without saying a word.

The neighbor continued. "We are going to come up here and sit on your porch while you go hunting for three hours. You are only going to get three bullets to take with you. And if you don't come back with enough stuff to eat for three days, we are never going to listen to you again!"

Old Man Hawkins knew he was caught. Well, if he was going to go down, he thought, he would do a good job of it!

He talked right back to his neighbors. "That suits me fine. Why, with three bullets and three hours, I should come back enough stuff to eat for three *weeks!* And what's more than that—I won't even use my own gun. I'll use any old gun you bring me."

This last part was a pretty good idea since he didn't even *have* a gun of his own.

And so, his three neighbors spent the next week telling everybody they knew about their plan and trying to come up with an interesting gun for Old Man Hawkins to use.

The Old Man himself spent the week worrying about what he was going to do when the actual time of the hunt arrived.

On Wednesday before the big Saturday, one of the three neighbors happened to be in town in Clyde doing a little shopping and telling everyone there about the plan for the great hunter. The blacksmith stopped him on the street and made him an offer.

"I've got the very gun he should use," the blacksmith offered. "Why, I made it myself! Yessir, and I am afraid to shoot it, too! My wife says I didn't get the barrel straight and that it would blow me to kingdom come. I don't think it would do that, but it might be interesting to see if Old Man Hawkins could do anything with it."

The offer was accepted on the spot, and the homemade gun was produced.

It was a long, smooth-bore, muzzle-loading affair, and the barrel did look like it took a significant slope toward the ground between the back and front sights. It *would be interesting to see what the old braggart could do with this.*

Finally Saturday morning arrived. Promptly at nine o'clock, the three neighbors stepped up on Old Man Hawkins's front porch and knocked on the door. They had the "homemade hog shooter" (as the blacksmith called it), three big homemade bullets, a powder horn full of black gunpowder, and the ramrod and patches to load it with.

Old Man Hawkins came to the door, looked at the long gun, and knew on the spot that he had no idea what to do even to begin to load the gun.

"Come in, boys," he led them inside. "You fellers got here a little earlier than I thought you would. Why, I've not even put on my hunting britches yet. I'll tell you what, just to be sure I don't miss any of my hunting time, why don't you load that thing up for me while I go in the back and put on my hunting britches."

He disappeared into the back room of the log house.

Old Man Hawkins only had one pair of britches—a pair of bib overalls—but he did pull them off, turn them wrongside out, and put them back on. Most of the time, though, he spent looking out through the crack in the door and watching his friends load the big hog shooter.

He saw them measure out a load of gunpowder using the cap on the powder horn. He saw them tamp down the powder before seating the bullet, using a patch of greasy cotton cloth to hold it securely in place and tapping it home with the ramrod. He saw them prime the pan on the flintlock gun, and he knew he could do the same for the last two shots.

Old Man Hawkins proudly stepped back out into the front room wearing his overalls inside out. "Ah, law!" he exclaimed. "This sure does look like a good day for a feller to go hunting if he knows what he's doing!" Thinking he was talking about himself, the neighbors began to grow excited that the great day had finally come to pass.

After telling them goodbye, Old Man Hawkins stepped out the door and down off the front porch. He did have a plan for what he was going to do first. Before anything else, he would get way out of sight! Then he would figure out what was supposed to come next. This much was a good plan to be sure.

The hillside in front of the Hawkins house sloped down to the Pigeon River, a good quarter-mile below. Old Man Hawkins walked down the hillside to the river. There at the water's edge, he stepped into a little homemade boat that everyone in the neighborhood used to cross back and forth over the river. He poled himself to the other side and got out of the boat.

Then he walked up a trail into the woods until he knew he was well out of sight of his porch, where a large group of neighbors was gradually gathering to visit until he returned later in the day.

Soon the Old Man came to a large stump where someone had cut down an old oak tree. He sat on the stump and began to talk to himself.

"Well...this looks like a pretty good place...for a feller to wait...for something to come along...that *wants* to get shot!" And he just sat there and waited.

As luck would have it, he heard a rustling in the leaves coming from up the trail. He glanced up there and saw a huge black bear coming down the trail and straight toward him. He slipped off the stump, laid the hog shooter across the top of it, and took aim at the bear.

When it was close enough, he pulled the trigger. *Blaamm!* the big gun went, and gave Old Man Hawkins a good kick in the shoulder. The barrel was, in fact, not straight, and the bullet only made it about half-way to the bear. The shot kicked up the dirt, and the bear turned on its heels and was gone.

"I'll be switched," Old Man Hawkins lamented. "That bullet was right on course, but it didn't go far enough. Why, those fellers that loaded this thing didn't know what they were doing. They must not have put enough gunpowder in it. I'll just have to use a lot more for the next shot!"

And so Old Man Hawkins reloaded the hog shooter just exactly the way he had seen it done through the crack in the door, except that this time, he put three full caps of powder down the barrel before seating the bullet on top of the load.

Ready for his second shot, Old Man Hawkins sat back down on the stump and waited.

Luck seemed to be with him, for he soon heard rustling in the trees straight ahead of where he was sitting. He looked up and saw a huge buck deer with a nice set of antlers to boot.

Old Man Hawkins slipped off and down behind the stump once again. He laid the hog shooter across the stump and, once again, took aim at his quarry.

When the deer seemed to be close enough, he pulled the trigger.

*BLLAAMMM!* The gun gave a kick which nearly dislocated the great hunter's shoulder.

The bullet did go farther this time—in fact, it went almost to where the deer was. But it hit the ground under the deer's belly, and the big buck was gone out of sight in a flash.

"I'll swan!" Old Man Hawkins lamented to himself. "That bullet didn't go far enough either. I just guess I didn't use enough gunpowder to get it on out there.

"Well, I've just got one shot left. I might as well make it a real good one!"

And so Old Man Hawkins emptied the entire contents of the powderhorn down the gunbarrel. Perched on top of what turned out to be six or seven inches of pure gunpowder was seated the last of the three homemade bullets. Now he was ready!

Old Man Hawkins knew that by now he had made so much noise he had surely scared off anything else which might live in this part of the woods. He set out walking back down toward the river to see whether he could scare up something else to shoot at with his last shot.

As he neared the river, he noticed that someone had come along and taken the little homemade boat back to the other side. He was disappointed, because now when he wanted to cross back over the river, he would have to wade through the water to get to the other side.

While he was trying to come up with a plan about what to do next, he began to hear a strange sound.

"Gobble, gobble, aah-bbleeeee!"

"Turkeys!" Old Man Hawkins said to himself. Why, even he knew that sound. He began to look around, sure that he would spot the big birds close enough for him to take a shot at them.

Finally he saw them. Across the Pigeon River, on a long, straight limb on the side of a big hickory tree, he counted twelve wild turkeys, shoulder to shoulder, in one long row!

He was excited now! "Surely," he thought to himself, "surely to goodness I can hit one out of twelve!"

Old Man Hawkins spread his feet apart to get a good hold on the earth. He put the gunstock against his shoulder and took aim at the turkeys.

When he was finally satisfied with his aim, he pulled the trigger.

*BLLAAMMM!* the awful gun echoed across the water.

Several things happened all at exactly the same time.

First, the hog shooter kicked Old Man Hawkins so hard it knocked him flat of his back on the riverbank and completely knocked the breath out of him. But then, he wouldn't have been able to breathe anyway because the air was so full of smoke and dust that nothing living could breath it. And he couldn't see anything because of the same dust and smoke, and he couldn't hear anything because his ears were still ringing with the sound of that great shot going off.

At last Old Man Hawkins got to where he could get his breath a little bit. When he looked down at the hog shooter, it was gone. The entire barrel of the long gun had exploded, and all that was left in the cradle of his arm was part of the wooden gunstock.

Slowly he raised up and looked across the river. He had *missed* every single one of those wild turkeys. There they all still sat, twelve in a row by actual count, still shoulder to shoulder on the limb of the hickory tree.

Old Man Hawkins was heartbroken. Here he was, about to be found out to be a person who didn't know the first thing about hunting. "I do reckon," he said out loud to himself, "that I am just going to have to go on back home and admit that I do not know what I am doing."

He started to try to get up off of the ground where he had fallen, and when he reached back to push himself up, he felt something furry. He looked behind him and saw that a groundhog must have been coming out of one hole and running toward another when Old Man Hawkins had pulled the trigger on the hog shooter. The groundhog had been exactly behind him, and when the hog shooter knocked him to the ground, he had sat on the groundhog and killed it dead.

"Well," his attitude was changing now, "look at this. Why, this must be lucky day! I have missed everything that I've shot at, but I won't go home empty-handed. I've got a good, fat groundhog to show!"

About that time he started hearing noises all around him. *Splash! Plop! Thump! Crash!* He looked around and suddenly realized what was happening.

When he had pulled that trigger for the last shot of the hog shooter, the gun barrel had, sure enough, exploded into a thousand pieces. At that very moment, a whole flock of wild geese had been flying by, way high in the sky overhead. Pieces of that exploding gun barrel had knocked the heads clean off of sixteen of those wild geese.

They had been so high in the sky that they were just now coming to the ground. Some were hitting in the river, some in the bushes, and some just flat on the ground.

Old Man Hawkins picked up a pole and fished out the ones which had landed in the river. When he had piled them all up, he counted them.

"This is my lucky day! Why, I've got a big fat groundhog *and* sixteen wild geese. But I guess I'll have to wade the river five or six times to get all of them to the other side."

Thinking there surely must be an easier way to get his big kill across the river than so many wet wading trips, Old Man Hawkins began to look around and think about the possibilities. When he saw there was a lot of dead wood, honeysuckle vines, and grape vines near where he was, he figured out what to do.

"I'll build a raft," he said to himself. "Then I'll only have to make one trip!"

And so he did. He gathered up a big pile of dead wood and began to tie it together with the vines. When he was finished, he had a crude-but-floating raft right there at the side of the water.

He loaded up the groundhog and the sixteen wild geese and he tried to get on board. The raft held the game very well, but it would not hold him. "Well," he thought, "I may have to wade and push the raft, but I'll only have to do it once."

And so, after pulling off his boots and putting them on the raft to keep dry, Old Man Hawkins waded down into the water and crossed the river, pulling the raft behind him.

Several times the water got so deep it almost came up over his head. Finally, he got close to the other bank. He got behind the raft and pushed it firmly up and onto the river-bank. Then he climbed onto the bank himself.

As soon as he left the water, Old Man Hawkins thought he felt something or somebody trying to tickle him to death all over. When he jumped around and didn't see anything, he realized what had happened.

As he had come through the waters of the Pigeon River, fish had swum into his clothes. They had gone in his britches legs, in the bib of his overalls, inside his shirt. He guessed they were trying to find a place to keep warm.

"This is my lucky day!" he said. "Why, I've caught fish without fishing!" With that, he threw his chest out proudly and two big fish, flopping around in the bib of his overalls, popped the buttons right off of his britches.

One button flew over behind a stump and killed a rabbit! The other button flew into a clump of broom sage and killed a quail! When Old Man Hawkins got through shaking the fish out of his overalls, he had twenty-two fish right there on the ground.

"Is this ever my lucky day!" he exclaimed once again. "I've got a fat groundhog, sixteen wild geese, twenty-two fish, a rabbit, and a quail, and I didn't shoot a single one of them!"

While he was trying to figure out a way to keep his overalls from falling down (now that he had lost the buttons in his game hunt), he heard the noise again: "Gobble, gobble, aah-bbleee!"

"Why," he thought, "that sounds like those same old turkeys. They sound like they're right here! Now, with all the noise I've made around here, why haven't they flown off somewhere, as skitterish as those things are?"

He looked around, and when he finally looked up, there he spotted the turkeys. They were sitting on that same hickory tree limb which was now right over his head. He couldn't believe they were just sitting there and not flying away.

Then Old Man Hawkins realized what had happened.

That last great shot, that last shot powered by six inches of black gunpowder, that shot had indeed missed every one of the turkeys—but it had hit the limb the turkeys were sitting on.

When that happened, the limb split, the turkeys' toes fell into the crack in the limb, and the limb smacked back together and caught all twelve of those turkeys right by the toes! They were trapped and couldn't get away.

"It *is* my lucky day! On top of everything else, I've got twelve, fresh wild turkeys—if I can figure out how to get them down!

Old Man Hawkins (partly because he had never owned a gun) was in the habit of carrying a short-handled axe in his belt just to make him feel good about himself. Now, he thought, that axe would come in handy, and he started to cut down the tree.

He didn't really know any more about cutting trees than he did about hunting. He chopped around and around the tree, one whack at a time and every time in a different place.

This would never have worked except that the tree was hollow, and before long the axe broke through into the hollow base, the tree listed to one side, and with a great smash, it fell to the ground. Old Man Hawkins was proud of himself…for a few moments.

For as the tree fell, two distinct things happened at once. From high up in the tree, he heard a loud OWWOWWOWW sound, and at the very same time, he felt something stinging him all over.

He ran for the river, took a big breath, and jumped into the water. He stayed under just as long as he could before breaking out of the water.

When he did, what he saw was a whole swarm of honey bees leaving that hollow tree. Why, the hollow tree must have been full of at least four or five hundred pounds of wild honey.

Then he realized what had made the OWWOWWOWW noise. The same old black bear he had shot at on the other side of the river, that very bear had swum over to this side and climbed up into this tree to get himself a snack of honey. When the tree was cut out from under him, there was nothing left for the bear to do but fall and fallen he had!

The old bear had hit the ground smack on the top of his head and his brains had flown out both ears. He was also, Old Man Hawkins noted, dead!

The Old Man came crawling up the riverbank, more amazed than ever. He said again. "This is my lucky day. Now I've got a groundhog, sixteen wild geese, twenty-two fish, a rabbit and a quail, a tree full of honey, twelve wild turkeys, and a bear with no brains!"

After reviewing this list again, he began to wonder how his turkeys had come down. So, he made his way toward the top of the tree to check on them.

The turkeys were just fine, still caught in the crack of the limb, but there was something else.

The buck deer Old Man Hawkins had shot at across the river had also swum over and was taking a nap in a thicket of bushes. When the tree fell, it killed the deer.

"A groundhog, sixteen wild geese, twenty-two fish, a rabbit and a quail, a tree full of honey, a bear with no brains, and a deer! This is enough," Old Man Hawkins thought. "I am going to quit looking around now, because if I keep looking, everything in these woods will be dead pretty soon!"

This was not just enough for three days, not just enough for three weeks, this was a lot more than enough for *three months!*

In spite of his great luck, Old Man Hawkins still did wish that he didn't have to carry all of this meat up the hill to his cabin. "There ought to be an easier way," he thought, remembering the raft.

As he glanced around, he spotted the little homemade boat. Whoever had come back across the river in it had left it right here. Old Man Hawkins looked at the seatless, flat-bottomed boat and thought, "That boat would make a good sled. I'll just load everything up and make one big pushing trip the hill."

And so it was done. He cut the section out of the tree which had the honey in it, left the limb on with the turkeys attached, and put it right in the back of the boat. The turkey limb faced the front, so that they could make shade on all the rest of the load.

Then he cleaned the groundhog and packed the meat in the bottom. He skinned (there was not time for picking feathers) the sixteen headless wild geese and packed them down there. He cleaned and scaled the fish, cleaned the rabbit and the quail, butchered the bear and the deer, and packed all that load of meat into the boat-sled.

All finished, he spread the bear skin over it to keep it fresh. He positioned the bear's head in the front, mouth propped open, so it would scare away anything that happened to try to get some of the load of meat.

Now, at least, it would only take one big push to get his kill home. He wished he could get some help with that.

Old Man Hawkins had put his boots back on and was just tying the laces when the idea hit him. "Rawhide!" He noticed the very laces he was tying, and commented to himself.

"Rawhide...these laces are rawhide, and I have an entire fresh deer hide just hanging there on the limb of that tree where the turkeys are riding.

"I think I will just make me a deerhide rope and try to get me some help to pull this load home." And so he set to work.

He cut the deer hide in strips and made holes in the ends of each one. Then he joined them by threading the next strip through a hole in the last and then back through itself. By the time he finished, Old Man Hawkins had made a rope he was sure would reach all the way from here to the house. He might get some help after all.

He fastened one end of the deerhide rope to the front of the boat, and he took the other end and started climbing the hill.

There was a great crowd of people gathered there now, waiting for his return. It turned out the fresh deerhide rope was a little shorter than he'd thought but still about right. The crowd watched while he stretched it until it reached the center post in the front porch. He tied the rope to the sturdy post, stepped up on the porch, sat down, and began to rock.

One of his neighbors finally asked, "Did you have any luck?"

Old Man Hawkins answered calmly, "I didn't do much with my first two shots, but I did right well with the last one."

"Well," said another neighbor impatiently. They'd been waiting a while to see Old Man Hawkins come home. "Where is it?"

"Oh, just be patient," the Old Man answered. "It will be along here directly."

The crowd watched, and Old Man Hawkins rocked, and the afternoon sun shone in on the hillside.

The hot sun began to dry out the fresh deerhide rope, and as the deerhide rope dried out, it began to shrink, and as the rope shrunk, it began to pull the entire boat-sled full of meat right up the side of the hill toward the house, without anybody having to do any work at all.

Of course, there was no one to guide the boat in the course of its journey, and from time to time, it would hit a rock or a stump which happened to be just exactly in its path. That wasn't much of a problem, though, because the turkeys were still on duty. Whenever the boat hit a stump or a rock, the *Whuump!* sound it made when it hit would scare the turkeys, who would flap their wings and fly the entire boat-sled full of meat right up in the air and over the obstacle. When it landed, it just kept coming, right on toward the house.

The entire assembled neighborhood watched the load come up the side of the hill and finally, into Old Man Hawkins's yard.

Once it had come about as far as it looked like it would, Old Man Hawkins took all the neighbors out to it and showed them the fruits of his last shot.

There the gathered people saw a groundhog, sixteen wild geese, twenty-two fish, a rabbit and a quail, a tree full of honey, twelve wild turkeys, a bear, and a deer!

The entire assembled neighborhood, with one voice, said, "This must have been your lucky day!"

It is also reported that Old Man Hawkins's neighbors never asked him to go hunting again because, they thought he *might* kill everything. It is *also* reported that Old Man Hawkins quit bragging after that. You might have *one* lucky day, he thought, but you better not count on having *two*!

# *Notes*

*I include this appendix in hopes of showing that family stories are usually joint efforts. Some are substantially the creation of one person. Others clearly have multiple personalities. All of them, though, have had have had a few chips carved by most everyone who ever regularly told them.*

## *RAINY WEATHER*
Uncle Frank always had a variety of foxhounds and they were the subject of much conversation. On several occasions, Uncle Frank was asked what happened to a particular dog.

At one such time, he told his questioner that the missing dog had trailed a fox until the dog was picked up on the Little Rock, Arkansas, watershed. He never got the dog back because he refused to pay the water pollution fine.

Another time, the answer was that the dog in question had trailed a fox until he was found in Baltimore, barking at a fur coat. This particular memory was the seed for this entire story.

The story itself gradually grew in being retold and retold until it had increased from five minutes to thirty minutes long.

Rainy Weather became a vehicle to carry everything wonderful about special hunting dogs which I could manage to fit together into one story.

## *UNCLE FRANK AND THE SOUTHERN BELLS*
Uncle Frank was often known to imitate the other tenants of his party line.

In this story, I created the Leatherwood sisters as vehicles for these memories and added the personality-building material and a bit of plot which seemed necessary to make the story work.

## UNCLE FRANK SAVES THE JOLLYS

In this story, I have taken two traditional themes often found in world folklore and have created the Phyleete Jolly family as the classical fools through whom the story functions.

The traditional themes are that of the fools who have never seen the moon and do not know what it is, and that of the fools who become separated and believe one of them to be lost because the "counter" never counts himself.

As the story exists now, Uncle Frank is not the source but a character in the story.

## WHATEVER HAPPENED TO THE JOLLYS?

The title of this story is the actual question I was often asked after telling the first of the Jolly stories. Since it needed to be answered, I created this story.

There is one variant of a traditional theme in the story: the trick of lengthening the rope to create the effect that the house has been moved. In some versions, the dog's rope is lengthened so that the dog catches the cat which thought it knew exactly how long the rope was.

## JOLLY OLD SAINT NICHOLAS

This story is almost purely traditional. The theme of following one's own footsteps in the snow occurs widely.

The original part of the story is simply my including it in the Jolly canon. I needed a funny Christmas story at the time.

## UNCLE FRANK INVENTS THE ELECTRON MICROPHONE

Uncle Frank and I conspired on this story, though the conspiracy occurred some years after his death. He invented the Jolly Cove echo chamber, and often told people about it. I invented the microphone so that the echo chamber could be proved useful.

The Ratherton boys are typical neighbors whose greatest talent is that they are nobody in particular.

## UNCLE FRANK LEARNS TO SPEAK POLISH

This story, too, is about half mine and half Uncle Frank's. Adam and Eve were real, and there were many events and adventures with them in addition to those used in the story.

I invented the Bible salesmen and inserted that segment, but Uncle Frank invented the Russian engineer and left him to the story.

## UNCLE FRANK AND THE CROWN FEED BOYS

The story Uncle Frank told the Crown Feed boys was a story he used to tell us, pretending that he actually couldn't read.

As the seed story seemed to need a larger setting, I created the Crown Feed Boys and the events of the sales visit as a larger matrix for the small initial story.

## UNCLE FRANK ALMOST BECOMES A DETECTIVE

This story was largely told as it stands here. My work with it has been to move from the form in which it was told among family to a form which created the world and characters for those who did not already know them.

## UNCLE FRANK CLEANS UP THE POST OFFICE

This story was substantially told in bare plot form by Uncle Frank. I have just smoothed it up a bit.

## LITTLE BUCHANAN OUTRUNS THE LAW

The last part of this story, that is, the part where Uncle Frank scares the boy and has him run from the law, comes from Uncle Frank.

The creation of the character and all the build-up about the driver's being an escaped prisoner are to get us to that conclusion.

## UNCLE FRANK AND THE SNAKE GUINEAS

Uncle Frank did tell this story, and it was published in the newspaper as written up by an unnamed young reporter.

## UNCLE FRANK AND THE TALKING CAT

There is a small memory of Uncle Frank reporting that a cat once talked to him and told him not to throw something at it, and that he thought the cat was a witch.

From that beginning point, the characters of Marshall and Anna were created, along with the traits and events which came from trying to do something with this small memory.

## AUNT ESTHER AND THE MISSING CATS

Aunt Esther did have two cats which disappeared. When asked what happened to them, she simply replied (using hand motions) that they climbed on one another's backs until they were out of sight.

With this beginning place I needed characters, motive, and outcome to make the story satisfactory.

I tried to put it together as a story which could be used with an audience of all ages.

## UNCLE GUDGER'S FIRST PET

The traditional story of the fish which stays out of the water until it forgets how to swim and then drowns is one of the most widespread tall-tale themes found in this country.

I first heard it from Uncle Gudger, and so I keep him with it. The setting and the events which lead up to the tragedy gradually grew after it was told and re-told and re-told...

## HOW TO GET RID OF AN OVERFED CAT

Uncle Gudger once asked if I had ever heard of the cat which disappeared and then came home with its head in its mouth. Of course, I had not, and was very disappointed when I learned that that's all there was to the story.

So, enter Livermush! I created the giant cat as something even a cat-lover might see the need to dispose of.

## OLD MAN HAWKINS'S LUCKY DAY

In my memory, this was truly my Father's favorite story. He told it again and again.

His version included different episodes from time to time. The usual ones were trapping the turkeys and cutting the tree onto the deer, and always pulling the sled home with the deerskin rope.

I use it to incorporate every miraculous hunt theme which I am possibly able to include in one story.